HOW TO SETTLE A GRUDGE MATCH

After Bruce and Susan's marathon back-gammon match, they were completely exhausted. The result—a tie. The solution—"A rematch!" they both shouted in unison.

Standing next to Bruce—possibly the cutest guy she'd ever seen—Susan suddenly felt lightheaded. And a second later Bruce had his arms around her holding her up.

"Are you going to faint to get out of kissing me?" Bruce asked gently.

Before Susan could answer, he pulled her tightly to him and kissed her. She closed her eyes. No more game-playing now. . . .

WILD MOVES

Campus Fever 8

WILD MOVES

by

Joanna Wharton

A SIGNET VISTA BOOK

NEW AMERICAN LIBRARY

PUBLISHER'S NOTE

This novel is a work of fiction. Names, characters, places, and incidents either are the product of the author's imagination or are used fictitiously, and any resemblance to actual persons, living or dead, events, or locales is entirely coincidental.

NAL BOOKS ARE AVAILABLE AT QUANTITY DISCOUNTS WHEN USED TO PROMOTE PRODUCTS OR SERVICES. FOR INFORMATION, PLEASE WRITE TO PREMIUM MARKETING DIVISION, NEW AMERICAN LIBRARY, 1633 BROADWAY, NEW YORK, NEW YORK 10019.

RL 5/IL 8 +

VISTA TRADEMARK REG.U.S.PAT.OFF. AND FOREIGN COUNTRIES REGISTERED TRADEMARK-MARCA REGISTRADA HECHO EN CHICAGO, U.S.A.

SIGNET, SIGNET CLASSIC, MENTOR, ONYX, PLUME, MERIDIAN and NAL BOOKS are published by New American Library, 1633 Broadway, New York, New York 10019

First Printing, November, 1986

1 2 3 4 5 6 7 8 9

PRINTED IN THE UNITED STATES OF AMERICA

Chapter 1

If Rachel doesn't stop that humming, I'm going to go out of my mind, Susan Radcliffe thought to herself.

Susan sat on the floor of the common room, which was one half of her Windsor Hall suite. Her books and notes were spread around her, but she wasn't in the mood to study. Through the door to the bedroom she could see her roommate, Rachel Pirnie, happily getting ready for her date with Scott Hammer. Susan took off her tortoiseshell glasses and stuck them on top of her head. Now Rachel was just a blurry form. Susan was nearsighted. When she removed her glasses, she couldn't see halfway across the room. Maybe she had to listen to Rachel, but she didn't have to look at her.

Susan's thoughts were interrupted by a knock at the door. Straightening the collar of the yellow and pink polka-dot turtleneck that she wore under her pink Hastings College pullover, she got up to open it.

"Hi, Susan. What's happening?" Susan's best friend, Daphne Riesling, strolled into the room, a cigarette case in one hand and an open beer in the other. She flopped gracefully into a chintz-covered armchair.

Susan and Daphne were often mistaken for sisters. Both were tall, blue-eyed, pretty, and model slim. But while Susan wore her straight pale hair in a long bob, Daphne's darker honey-blond hair had recently been cut and permed into a wavy shag—"my new mane," as Daphne liked to call it.

"I'll tell you what's happening," Susan said, settling on the couch. She jerked her thumb in Rachel's direction. "Pirnie is a walking happy face, that's what."

Daphne grimaced and then took a swig of her beer. "How nice for her."

Rachel finished putting a barrette in her gleaming copper-colored hair and walked into the room. "Of course I'm happy. I have a lot to be happy about." She turned and glanced at the full-length mirror on the bedroom door. Her black leather pants and red silk blouse hugged her body. The outfit had cost a bundle and looked it. Rachel's wealthy family provided an ample clothing budget and Rachel used every bit of it—just one of the many reasons she drove Susan and Daphne crazy.

"So things are really going your way, huh?" Daphne asked, overly sweet.

"You know they are. A new boyfriend, a new sorority." Then she paused. "But no matter how good things are, I guess there always has to be one fly in the ointment." Rachel looked directly at Daphne. Slowly her gaze shifted to Susan. "Make that two flies."

Daphne ignored this. "Doesn't Rachel look nice today?" she said cattily to Susan. "I don't know about the blouse, though. With Rachel's red hair and all . . ."

Susan pretended to consider the appropriateness of the clothes Rachel was wearing. Then she shook her head, her fair hair moving in a perfect arc. "No, I don't think it works. Especially on top of those pants."

"A little geeky?" Daphne suggested. Susan nodded her head in agreement. Susan watched Rachel closely for evidence that they were getting to her.

But instead of looking bothered, Rachel just laughed. "Well, I'm sorry you don't like the outfit," she said. "I'm sure Scott will." She gave Daphne a big smile. "It's one of his favorites."

Her zinger hit home. Daphne had once been very interested in Scott Hammer, but he had dropped her the moment Rachel came on the scene.

As Daphne lowered her eyes, Rachel turned her attention to Susan. "And you know, Susan," she continued conversationally, "when I was over at the Gamma house the other day, everyone raved about the way I looked."

Now it was Susan's turn to look away. Both Susan and Daphne had been wild to get into Gamma Gamma Phi. Not only did the Gammas have the reputation for being cool sophisticates, they catered to girls who shared Susan and Daphne's upper-class backgrounds.

Susan had grown up in Lake Forest, Illinois, a luxurious suburb on the shores of Lake Michigan. Her father was a prominent banker who made the hour-long commute into Chicago from the family's sprawling Victorian home. Mrs. Radcliffe died when Susan was only seven, but a year or so later her father remarried an elegant blond woman named Gloria, and that's when Daphne became a part of Susan's life. Gloria and Daphne's mother, Jean, had known each other forever. Naturally they wanted Susan and Daphne to be best buddies too. Both Gloria and Mrs. Riesling saw to it that their daughters were in all the right places. Susan and Daphne had attended the same exclusive Briarwood County day school, made their debuts at the same cotillion, and had both applied to Mt. Holyoke College. They had both been turned down.

Susan was secretly relieved by Holyoke's rejection. She hoped it might pave the way for her to attend a large, midwestern university like Wisconsin or Michigan State. But Daphne had insisted that if they couldn't get into Mt. Holyoke, they should still be in Massachusetts because there were such great colleges (and great guys) in the Boston area. When they were both accepted at Hastings College, a pretty little school just outside the city, Daphne had been ecstatic. Susan had put up a token resistance, but as was usually the case, she gave in to Daphne, especially after Gloria and Mrs. Riesling agreed that Hastings would be an acceptable choice.

As far as Susan was concerned, though, things had not been that great since she and Daphne had arrived at Hastings and moved into Windsor Hall.

It started with the room. Susan thought she'd love living with her best friend, but those first few months were filled with squabbles. Sure, they had pulled together for Daphne's schemes, or whenever the dorm ganged up on them, but finally Susan decided the only way to stay friends with Daphne was to move out. She begged Rachel to let her move into the empty place in her suite— little dreaming she'd be begging her to switch back a few months later.

Now Susan was looking forward to living with someone who actually liked her. Certainly, none of the other Windsorites fit that description.

Almost from the first there had been problems with the other girls. A disagreement with Windsor Hall's resident track star, Cathy Thomas, had resulted in Rachel organizing the silent treatment against them— until Susan was forced to apologize, in *public*. Then there was the whole Gamma thing. Susan dreaded what Gloria would say when she found out the Gammas didn't want her. The dating scene had been looking pretty bleak, too. The last thing Susan needed was Rachel Pirnie rubbing her nose in her social defeat.

"So, what are you two up to tonight?" Rachel asked pleasantly, pressing her advantage.

"We have studying to do," Daphne answered, sullenly sipping her drink.

"Oh, that's good," Rachel said approvingly. "You know my motto: if you can't date, study."

"Shouldn't you be hitting the books too?" Susan asked pointedly. "Your grades haven't been all that hot."

Rachel pretended to consider this seriously. "That's true," she admitted, "but of course, now that I'm a Gamma pledge, I have to keep my grades up. And the Gammas have a terrific tutoring program to make sure their pledges do all right."

"Swell," Daphne muttered under her breath.

"And Scott knows so much about literature," Rachel went on sweetly, "I'm sure he's going to be a big help."

"I don't know if even Scott has that much patience," Daphne shot back.

Susan gave a small sigh. These verbal battles were second nature to her but, to tell the truth, she was getting tired of all the bickering. She wished for once that Daphne would just let it be. But Daphne wasn't like that.

"Right, Susan?" Daphne's insistent voice interrupted her thoughts.

"What?" Susan asked, momentarily lost.

Daphne directed her words to Susan, but her eyes were on Rachel. "I said, don't you think Rachel better have another guy in reserve? I mean, Scott doesn't know her all that well. And to know her well is to dislike her." Rachel reddened angrily. Finally happy, Daphne winked at Susan. "Don't you think?"

"*I* think Rachel ought to get downstairs," Susan broke in before Rachel could really explode. "She doesn't want to keep Loverboy waiting."

Both Rachel and Daphne gaped at Susan, but Rachel recovered first. "My, my," she said, lightly, "I think for once in her life Susan is right." She grabbed her red leather purse off the coffee table and checked for her keys as she went to the door. "Take a break from your studying around eleven, girls, and think of me. That's when Scott and I should be pulling in to that deserted parking lot behind the geology building." She flashed Daphne a wicked grin and sailed out. Daphne threw a slipper at the door as it slammed shut behind her.

"That stupid cow," Daphne said, rising to look for an ashtray. "She is going to be so sorry."

Susan stretched out over the length of the couch. "Yeah, and how are you going to accomplish that?" she asked.

"We. We are going to do it."

"Oh, I don't know," Susan said wearily.

Daphne shot a furious look in her direction. "What is it with you tonight, Radcliffe? You just sit there like some lump while that dumb redhead insults us, and then you don't even pay attention or support me when I try to make points for our side."

"That's not true," Susan defended herself. "I'm the one who mentioned grades."

Daphne lit her cigarette and took a long drag. "Yeah, great. That gave her the opportunity to tell us that the Gammas and Scott would be helping her every step of the way."

"So I said the wrong thing. I'm sorry."

"All right," said Daphne, somewhat mollified. She grabbed an ashtray and sat back down in the pink chintz chair. "It doesn't really matter, anyway, because I am going to get that girl and the Gammas too."

Susan sat straight up. "You do have a plan, don't you?"

"Maybe," Daphne answered coyly.

"Well, what is it?" Susan demanded, suddenly awake. There was nothing like a plan of Daphne's to get her blood racing. Ever since they were little, Daphne had come up with the most outrageous ideas. Susan never could resist going along. When they were ten, Daphne had made every girl in ballet class jealous by pretending Baryshnikov was a close personal friend of their families. At fourteen, she convinced their parents they all needed to go to Europe for the summer. High school provided ample opportunities to bedevil teachers, steal other girls' boyfriends, party hard on weekends, and get away with as much as was humanly possible without their families finding out. If anyone could discover a way to shake things up at Hastings and improve their deadly situation, it was Daphne.

"So spill it," Susan prompted.

"I haven't quite got something for Pirnie yet," Daphne admitted, "but I do have a way to get the Gammas."

"Really?"

"When we were being rushed by the Gammas, do you remember hearing about a Mrs. Gregory Dunbar?"

"Yeah, I do. She went to Hastings about a million years ago, right?"

"Right. And she donated lots of money to the Gamma house. Every other thing they showed us had a plaque that said, 'A Gift of Mrs. Gregory Dunbar.'"

"I guess they did, but so what?" Susan asked, puzzled.

Daphne smiled slyly. "What if Mrs. Dunbar wrote a letter saying that Susan Radcliffe and Daphne Riesling were two of the finest young ladies she ever had the good fortune to know, and that she certainly hoped they'd be inducted as pledges at her sorority."

"But why would she do that?" Susan asked blankly. "She doesn't even know us."

"Oh Susan," Daphne groaned, stubbing out her cigarette. "Mrs. Dunbar wouldn't write it, we would."

"And they'd believe it?"

A secret smile played around Daphne's lips. "They would if it were written on official Gamma Gamma Phi stationery."

"You have some?"

"Not yet, but I'll get it," Daphne said with determination.

Susan got up off the couch and began pacing the room. "I don't know, Daphne. Where would it get us?"

"Are you dense, or what?" Daphne asked, curling a strand of dark blond hair around her finger. "If the Gammas' most ardent supporter wants us, they'll have to reconsider us as pledges."

"Oh, I don't know . . ."

"They will," Daphne insisted. "But even if they don't—*if*—then at least they'll be all upset because they've gotten on the wrong side of their precious Mrs. Dunbar."

Susan stopped pacing and nervously started rearranging the Hastings knick-knacks on the shelf over her desk. "It doesn't sound like it will work, Daphne. I mean, you don't even have the stationery . . ."

"I said I'd get it."

" . . . and if you do, and the Gammas find out, we could get in trouble."

"Trouble? So what? When did we ever worry about getting into trouble?"

"True," Susan admitted. "I don't know, I guess I'm just not in the mood."

"Well, excuse me. I'm very sorry you're not in the mood," Daphne said, her voice dripping with sarcasm, "but I think it's a damn good idea."

"Look, Daphne . . ." Susan tried to placate her. She hated it when Daphne got angry.

"Don't 'Look, Daphne' me," she retorted, cutting Susan off. "I don't need to hear that crap."

Betty Berke opened the door a crack and stuck her head inside. "Ladies, ladies, people can hear you in the hall."

"Oh great," said Daphne, lighting another cigarette. "If it isn't Betty Boop."

Little Betty Berke was Daphne's roommate. Short, with curly, carrot-colored hair and an infectious grin, she looked younger than the other girls and often acted that way. Betty had spent most of first semester hung up on Mitch Goudy, sure that they would get married. That is, until Mitch had a fling with another girl and broke Betty's heart. Betty had spent a lot of time in her suite since she'd sworn off men. But at least she was willing to trade rooms so Susan and Daphne could be together again. If only Rachel would stop insisting it was too late in the year to switch, everything would be fine.

"Can I come in?" Betty asked in a bouncy tone. Daphne turned away. With her bubbly personality and kind nature it was hard not to like Betty. In fact Daphne was the only person Susan knew who really tried to dislike Betty.

Susan was generally rather fond of Betty, but she wasn't up for seeing her right now. "What is it?" she snapped, too impatient to be nice.

"They posted the notice for the Nightingale auditions," said Betty, stepping gingerly into the room. "It's tomorrow night." The Nightingales were Hastings' prestigious women's chorale group. Susan, Daphne, and Betty all had hopes of getting in, and they had been waiting for the audition call for weeks.

"Well, it's about time," Daphne said.

"I'll say," Susan agreed. "I thought they were going to make us wait forever." She, for one, would be glad to hear the end of Daphne's griping and rehearsing. It wasn't that Daphne didn't have a nice voice. She'd have to, what with her mother having been a real live professional singer—before she got married. It was just that Susan had an aversion to being serenaded with *a cappella* renderings of top 40 songs in public. Daphne was her best friend and all, but Susan wished she'd learn to sing in the shower like everyone else.

"Do you have your audition songs ready?" Betty asked.

"Of course," Susan answered.

"What are you singing?"

" 'Summertime,' from *Porgy and Bess.*"

Susan knew the haunting Gershwin song suited her soprano voice beautifully.

"What about you, Daphne?"

" 'Like a Virgin,' " Daphne smirked.

"You wouldn't!" Betty was shocked.

"Wouldn't I?" Of course she wouldn't. Susan knew Daphne planned to sing a very sedate version of "The Way We Were." She wasn't Barbra Streisand, but Susan had to agree she did pretty well with it, a terrific job, to hear Daphne tell it.

Betty waited for someone to ask about her selection. When no one did, she told them anyway. "I'm going to sing 'Beautiful Dreamer,' by Stephen Foster."

" 'Beautiful Dreamer'?" Susan snickered.

"What's wrong with 'Beautiful Dreamer'?" Betty asked indignantly. "It's an old favorite."

"It's old, all right," Daphne said.

"And a favorite . . . of our grandmothers. Make that our great-grandmothers," Susan said.

Betty looked at her feet. Susan was suddenly sorry for baiting her. Poor thing. You'd think after a term of living with Daphne, she'd have given up on trying to make friends with her.

"I hear the Nightingales only have a few places open," Susan said conversationally, ignoring Daphne's glare.

Betty nodded emphatically. "That's what scares me."

Daphne laughed scornfully and went over

to the wrought-iron magazine rack; she picked up a *Vogue*. "I guess some of us have things to be scared of." Susan stared in disbelief at Daphne's cool pose. Could this be the same Daphne who'd been singing Phil Collins tunes on the bus yesterday, trying to get her voice in shape?

"What's the story on Jorge?" Betty asked.

That caught Daphne's attention. Everyone was interested in Jorge Marquez, the Nightingales' choirmaster and faculty adviser. His dark, Latin looks were the talk of the campus. "What about Jorge, Betty?"

"He'll be conducting the auditions, don't you think?"

"Of course. Why wouldn't he?"

"I don't know. I thought maybe he'd be out of town or something."

Daphne snorted. "He has to be there, Betty. He makes the decisions, although I guess he gets some advice from Nancy Gurney," she said, mentioning the name of the Nightingale president, who was also a Gamma Gamma Chi.

Betty looked miserable. With her hair pulled back in a ponytail and wearing her favorite outfit, a T-shirt and Oshkosh overalls, she seemed all of ten years old. "I knew that. It's just that he makes me so nervous."

"Then why not forget the whole thing?" Daphne suggested.

"Oh, I couldn't do that. I've always wanted

to be a Nightingale. Ever since I read about them in the Hastings catalog."

Amazed, Susan watched Daphne shake her head at Betty's confession—even though Daphne had told Susan almost the same thing just the other day; well, actually, what she'd said was, "I knew the Nightingales were dying for a singer like me from the moment I saw the catalog."

"Maybe we could go over the auditions together. You, me and Susan, I mean," Betty was saying.

"Just the Three Musketeers?" Daphne snickered.

"We should leave about seven," said Betty, but before she could finish making plans, Cathy Thomas came to the door.

"Telephone for you, Susan."

"For me? I'm not expecting any calls." She frowned at Daphne, who delicately shrugged her shoulders.

"Well, what should I tell him?" Cathy asked impatiently.

"It's a him? I'll take it." Susan felt a thrill of excitement. Could it possibly be that hunk from Psych 101, Randy Applewood?

"Did you get a name?" she asked Cathy when they reached the hall.

"Some guy with a Bulgarian accent, sounded like. He said something about it being that time again."

"Bruce," Susan groaned, collapsing against the wall, just short of the phone table. He meant it was time to ask her out. Again.

"Didn't sound like a 'Bruce' to me," Cathy shrugged, walking off before Susan could ask her to get rid of him.

Bruce Shetland. Susan shook her head. How could she relate seriously to someone who wore ties and bowling shirts—at the same time? Even if he was kind of cute. Well, it was too late now. She'd have to talk to him.

"Hello, Bruce?" she said, gingerly lifting the receiver.

"Ow-wooo," Bruce howled like a wolf.

"Would you be quiet!" Susan hissed. "The whole dorm will hear you."

"Susan, Susan, Susan," Bruce scolded. "Your upper-class mentality is showing again. Zee gut doktor ist goink to haff to find a cure for dis."

Susan sniffed. "Oh, really? Is that why you're still calling me after all the times I've turned you down. You want to cure my 'upper-class mentality'?"

"Perhepps," Bruce conceded, and then dropped his Dr. Freud act. "You ought to thank me for fighting the good fight. Most social reformers would take one look at that tidy blond hair and those tortoiseshell glasses and write you off as a hopeless prep. I, on the other hand, am determined to see you become all that you can be."

Susan could feel the steam rising to her ears. "I'll bet you think I think you're just kidding," she snapped. "I'll bet you think I ought to think you're doing me a favor."

"Whew," Bruce whistled. "I think you think too much about what I'm thinking about what you're thinking to think you really hate me as much as you think."

"I never said I hated you—"

"Ah-hah! So you will go out with me?"

"Ohhh," Susan growled. "Why do you have to be so weird?"

"If I weren't so weird, I wouldn't be so charming."

"If you weren't so weird, I wouldn't have to be ashamed to be seen with you."

" 'Ashamed to be seen with me,' " Bruce gasped in a high falsetto. "If that's not the snootiest thing I've ever heard. Ja, ja. The doktor can see your condition ist goink to rekvire months of intensive personal care."

"No, thanks. I'd rather stay hopeless." Susan's voice was firm, but she was smiling to herself. She heard Bruce sigh heavily on the other end.

"All right," he said. "I'll surrender my quest to play Higgins to your Doolittle."

"You will?" Susan felt unaccountably disappointed.

"Yes. From now on, I'll only appeal to your baser instincts. No—don't argue. You beat me down. I no longer have any integrity left."

"What are you talking about?"

Bruce's voice lowered conspiratorially. "I'm talking dinner here, Susan. Candlelight and wine lists. French cuisine. Waiters with dishtowels draped over their arms."

"Those aren't dishtowels," Susan corrected.

"Whatever they are—you'll have them. We're talking appetizer *and* dessert, Susan. Not to mention refills on coffee."

"We-ell," Susan wavered, tempted. It had been a long time since she'd been anywhere nice—anywhere at all, in fact. One evening with Bruce might even be fun. Compared to another dateless weekend at Windsor Hall, anyway. Then again, accepting would be like admitting Bruce was right about her. He was bound to rub her face in it.

"As a matter of fact," she said finally, "I'm busy that night."

"What night would that be?" Bruce asked archly.

Susan giggled, suddenly realizing he hadn't named a night.

"Ah, a good sign. Laughing at your own mistakes. This must mean you accept."

"It means I'll think about it," she said.

"Good as a 'yes' in my book," Bruce crowed. "Saturday night, seven o'clock. Dress to kill or be killed." Then he hung up before she had a chance to protest.

Still smiling to herself, Susan slipped back into the suite and headed toward the bedroom. Daphne followed her and sat on Rachel's bed.

"So who was that?" Daphne asked, finishing off her beer.

"Bruce Shetland."

Daphne hooted. "Him again? Doesn't he ever give up?"

"Hope springs eternal, I guess." Susan slipped off her turtleneck and jeans, revealing an expensive silk and lace teddy. "Besides, it's sort of flattering. He is kind of cute."

"Weird, you mean."

"Eccentric," Susan said as she slipped on a blue silk kimono. She was surprised to hear herself defending him.

"So what did he want?"

Susan picked up a cotton pad, sprinkled it with lotion, and began removing her eye makeup. "To take me out on Saturday."

"I hope you said no."

"Actually, I said maybe," Susan admitted.

Daphne looked shocked. "But why? You don't want to hang out with someone who divides his time between reading religious books and reading racing forms."

"He's interested in lots of things. So what?"

"Frankly, Susan, he's not our kind. I'm surprised you'd even consider him."

"Daphne, lately I can't get a date with 'our' kind or anyone else's kind."

"Well, you still shouldn't lower your standards," Daphne said virtuously. "I won't let you. People would talk."

"I doubt that."

Daphne played her trump card. "What would Gloria say?"

Gloria would hate it, Susan thought. Neither of her parents would like the idea of

her going out with an eccentric nobody.
Maybe it wasn't such a good idea to date
Bruce, after all.

Daphne pushed her point. "Are you really
that hard up?"

Susan gave in. "I guess not. You're right,
Daphne. When he calls back, I'll tell him I
can't make it."

Daphne smiled her first real smile of the
evening. "Good girl."

Chapter 2

Susan threw her geology book down on her rumpled bed and walked over to her window. She had been feeling so restless lately, she really wished something would happen. Something good, she silently amended. She was getting a little tired of all the tension around Windsor Hall.

As she gazed out the window, Susan noticed a solidly built guy with a shock of blond hair walking on the sidewalk below. Randy Applewood! Quickly, she let the ruffled curtain fall back into place.

Randy was the fullback of the Hastings football team. He was in two of Susan's classes and she spoke to him at every opportunity—not that he seemed to notice. She'd been about to give up on him when, just a few days ago, he had borrowed her psych notes. When he returned them, he had muttered something about giving her a call. Susan was almost afraid to believe him.

With good cause, apparently. She peeked back out the window. Randy was gone. He hadn't been on his way to see her after all. She threw herself back on the bed and stared at the ceiling. Oh well, she thought, at least I have a date with Bruce Shetland . . . if I want it.

Funny—Susan had been convinced she felt some kind of electricity the first instant she'd ever seen Bruce. Which just went to show you how wrong first impressions could be.

It was back on the first day of classes. Susan thought she'd memorized where all her courses were, but finding Econ 11B seemed hopeless. Five minutes before class, she'd reached the place clearly marked Grey Hall on her campus map. It was nothing but a big muddy hole.

She was just telling herself not to cry in public when, suddenly, someone was singing the Yale drinking song—right in her ear.

" 'We are poor little lambs, who have gone astray.' "

Susan's head snapped around; she found herself peering into a pair of enormous brown eyes. That was when she'd felt it, the electric connection. The singer's expression was wry, even mocking, but those eyes—just like a puppy dog's. It was a moment before Susan noticed he was wearing a red-and-black fox-hunting jacket and a baseball cap with "Sam's Bodyshop" stenciled on it.

"Are you looking for Grey Hall by any chance?" he asked when he realized she'd been struck dumb.

"How did you—"

"It's a conspiracy," he whispered. "The dean commissions the maps and then, secretly, in the dead of night, he has the buildings moved."

Susan laughed, a wave of relief washing over her. "And do you know where he might have moved my class?"

Her rescuer resettled the visor of his cap. "My guess is around the next corner to the Stadtler building." He winked at her. "I see someone didn't read the teeny-weeny footnote at the bottom of her schedule."

Susan sheepishly shook her head.

"Poor little lamb," he clucked. "But, never fear. I, Bruce Shetland, am available to shepherd you to your next class. Get it? Little lamb. Shetland. Shepherd. Shetland the shepherd."

Susan snorted, which seemed to delight Bruce.

"I love girls who snort! Even when they don't tell me their names."

"Oh. Susan. Susan Radcliffe." Susan stuck out her hand, which he shook and then wrapped firmly around his elbow.

"Radcliffe," Bruce mused as he led her to the Stadtler building. "Sounds quite hoity-toity. I ought to warn you, I have this thing about *Social Register*-type girls. Love to corrupt their morals."

"What if they don't have any morals?" Susan asked coyly, feeling very pleased with herself. Here it was, her first real day of freshman year and already a cute male person was escorting her to class.

Her pleasure faded a little, though, when she saw the looks Bruce's outrageous attire inspired. Had that pretty brunette been laughing at his pink hightops? Was that jocky-looking guy wondering what a girl like Susan was doing with a wacko like Bruce? Or worse, did he think she looked like the kind of girl who belonged with wackos?

Susan forced herself to keep up her end of Bruce's lightning-fast conversation—which had moved from debutantes to détente to doughnuts in the space of a few minutes. By the time Bruce deposited her at Stadtler, she felt shamefully relieved. That shame made her answer more nicely than she might have when Bruce told her he'd be calling her.

Since then, Susan had had a war with herself about turning down his periodic invitations. He was sort of attractive and his style was, well, original. She never had to worry about making small talk since Bruce knew something about everything. When he wasn't being completely freaky, he could be very amusing.

If only he wasn't such an oddball loner type, he'd be perfect. As it was, though, he was hardly the type she could bring home, not like the boys she had gone to school and dances with. They'd all been clean-cut, wealthy, and safe. Daphne was probably right. It was not a good idea to get mixed up with Bruce Shetland. He was too unpredictable. Too embarrassing.

Susan's train of thought was broken by Daphne bursting into the room, her cheeks red and her eyes bright. "I got it, I got it," she whispered.

Susan took in Daphne's outfit in a glance. Black sweater, black pants, and a black leather jacket. "Daphne," said Susan, sitting up. "Are you in mourning for somebody?"

Daphne threw herself down on the floor and leaned against the bureau. "Don't be ridiculous," she said, breathing heavily. "This is my cat-burglar outfit. You know I always like to dress for the occasion."

"What in the world is the occasion?"

With a sly smile, Daphne reached for the purse she'd unceremoniously dropped on the floor. She extracted a few pieces of heavy white linen paper and an envelope, and handed them to Susan. "I did it."

Susan's heart dropped when she examined the pages. Gamma Gamma Chi stationery. Now for sure Daphne would want to go ahead with her silly plan. "You actually snuck inside the Gamma house and got this?"

"Yep. Say, do you have anything to drink around here? I could use something to mellow me out."

"This isn't a liquor store, Daphne."

"Didn't you say Pirnie keeps a bottle of Jack Daniel's in her closet?"

The last thing Susan wanted was Daphne

drinking Rachel's liquor. "She finished it. Now tell me what happened."

"Well, I remembered that there was a Gamma pledge meeting this afternoon, so I knew they'd all be occupied. I walked over to Greek Street and just kind of wandered around until it looked like all the Gammas were inside. Then I snuck up to the window and peeked into the living room."

"You didn't!"

"Of course, I did," Daphne said practically. "I had to make sure they weren't still roaming around the house. But don't worry, they were all sitting in a cozy little circle having their meeting, including Mrs. Martin, the housemother."

"So what did you do?"

"I tried the back door. It was open, so I went inside."

"And no one saw you?" Susan asked incredulously.

Daphne laughed. "Actually, someone did. This guy John Reed who work/studies as their kitchen help. He was setting the table when I walked by. I told him I was from Many Happy Returns, the gift store, and I was supposed to leave a present in the housemother's office. He very kindly pointed me in the right direction." Daphne tossed her head. "Men can be so handy. Anyway, after that little scare, you can bet I was into that desk and out with the stationery in a flash."

Susan shook her head. As usual she was in awe of Daphne's bravery. Bravery with a dash of stupidity thrown in. "Boy, you were really lucky."

"Not lucky, smart. Now all I have to do is figure out how to trash Rachel."

There was a dangerous glint in Daphne's eye that Susan had seen too many times before. She sighed to herself. Here we go again. "I'm sure you'll come up with something," she responded wearily.

Daphne rubbed her hands together. "You can bet it'll be something devious, too. Meanwhile, why don't we write the letter from Mrs. Dunbar now?"

"Yeah, but tonight's the Nightingale audition," Susan quickly protested. "I want to spend some time getting ready."

Daphne got up and dusted off her pants. "Yeah, I want to wash my hair too." She walked over to Susan's closet and plucked out a blue-and-white cotton sweater. "Things like this would be much more fun to get ready for if we were living together. I still think there's gotta be a way we could switch rooms."

"It never seems to work out," Susan said guardedly. Actually, she was beginning to feel relieved that she and Daphne weren't roommates anymore. She hardly dared admit it to herself, but Daphne's friendship was beginning to get just a little bit suffocating. Feeling disloyal, Susan changed the subject. "Are you as nervous as I am about the audition?"

"No way," Daphne said with false bravado, holding the sweater up to her and looking in the mirror. "We've got it made. Riesling and

Radcliffe, stars of the Briarwood Girls Glee Club."

"The competition is going to be a lot stiffer here."

An anxious look crossed Daphne's face, but just as quickly disappeared. Why couldn't she just admit she was scared? "We're destined to make it," she said, trying to keep her voice light. "How could the daughter of the great Jean Riesling accomplish any less?" She reconsidered the checked sweater. "I'm sorry, Susan, this is really ugly."

"So don't wear it."

"Haven't you got anything decent in here?" Daphne asked, putting back the offending garment.

"Check out Rachel's side of the closet. She's the one with all the wonderful clothes."

Daphne started rummaging through Rachel's clothes. "Yeah, just the sort of outfits the Gamma girls go for. But, you know, if that letter works, it could be Rachel will get squeezed off the pledge list. Then she'll have no place to wear these lovely frocks."

"What lovely frocks?" Rachel asked curiously as she entered the room.

Susan paled and glanced over at Daphne, who looked equally taken aback. Noticing the stationery scattered around her, Susan casually picked it up and turned it facedown in her lap. "We were just saying what a great dresser you are, that's all."

Rachel gave them a suspicious look. "Gee, I

don't remember getting any compliments from you two lately, especially behind my back."

Daphne gave a small chuckle. "Well, maybe there was an ulterior motive, Rachel."

"I should have guessed."

Daphne grabbed a checked blouse and a white silk shell from Rachel's side of the closet and held them in front of Rachel's face. "I need something to wear tonight. You know, to the Nightingale audition. Can I borrow one of these?" Daphne babbled. While she was distracting Rachel, Susan leaned over and stuck the stationery in her desk drawer.

Rachel took the two blouses out of Daphne's hands and put them back in the closet. "Sorry, I'm not in the habit of lending things to people who hate my guts. You know how it is."

"Sure," said Daphne uncomfortably. "So I guess I'll go get ready. See you later, Susan."

"Later." She watched as Daphne almost ran out of the suite. Now what should she say to Rachel? As usual she was left to clean up Daphne's dirty work. Awkwardly, Susan got off her bed and walked into the common room. To her surprise, Rachel followed.

"I suppose you think I should have loaned her a blouse, right?" Rachel asked, a touch combatively.

"No," Susan replied honestly, "not if you didn't want to."

Rachel went around the room picking up

crumpled candy wrappers and Styrofoam cups, clutter that Susan honestly never noticed until she saw Rachel throwing it out. "I'm not a patsy, you know," Rachel said.

Susan felt ashamed. "I know," she muttered, and then felt disloyal. Being Daphne's friend could be so confusing.

Rachel stopped cleaning and looked at her. "Susan, there's something I've wanted to say to you for a long time. Maybe this is my chance. I know we had some problems early in the term, but we were getting along better until this stuff with the Gammas and Scott came up."

Susan was surprised that Rachel would be so candid. She didn't know what to say.

"I hate living in an armed camp. Do we really have to go on like this?"

"I . . . I guess not."

"I don't think we're going to be best friends, but at least we can be civil. It would make things more tolerable, wouldn't it?"

Susan was far more used to sarcasm than honesty. It caught her off guard. "Well, yeah. I guess we don't have to be at each other's throats all the time."

"Then we'll just cool the hostility?"

"Uh, okay. We can try that." Susan swallowed hard. Daphne was going to kill her.

"So, are you two ready?" Susan, dressed for the audition, came into Daphne's and Betty's bedroom. She had been in a quandary about her outfit and finally decided on a

Laura Ashley blouse with muttonchop sleeves and a black flared linen skirt. She hoped Jorge Marques would find it wildly romantic.

Daphne, dressed in a hot-pink camp shirt and black wool slacks, was sitting at her desk chair sipping something out of a plastic glass. "I'm ready," she said, "but Berke disappeared into the hall bathroom an hour ago and she hasn't been heard from since."

Susan nervously looked at her watch. "She better hurry up, or we're going to have to leave without her. By the way, as long as we're alone, take this." Susan shoved a white canvas bag she'd brought with her into Daphne's hands.

Daphne peeked inside and grinned when she saw the Gamma Gamma Chi stationery. "Thanks," she said as she shoved the bag under the bed. "That was close this afternoon, huh?"

"Too close."

"Oh come on," Daphne scoffed. "Where's your sense of adventure? Now, if we were living together, we could really come up with some great stuff."

Susan didn't even want to consider what those plans might be. She almost wished—no, she *did* wish she could just finish out the year with Rachel. Especially if Rachel was on the level about cooling things down. Boy, she was going to have to make sure Daphne didn't discover she and Rachel had called a truce, though. Daphne would consider that the ultimate betrayal. Well, with any luck, she wouldn't find out. Susan would just be polite to Rachel in the privacy of their room and kind of avoid her when Daphne was around. Oh, why did it have to be like this with Daphne, Susan thought, unexpectedly near tears. Why did Daphne's enemies have to be *her* enemies? What would make her drop this stupid vendetta against the Gammas and Rachel?

Daphne looked at her curiously. "Hey, a penny for your thoughts."

"Uh, just thinking about the audition. There's only four freshman places open, you know."

Daphne shrugged. "I told you, we're shoo-ins." Susan thought she saw her lips tremble as she took another sip of her drink.

"Hey, can I have some of that? My mouth is dry already."

"Sure, go ahead."

Susan sputtered as the burning liquor ran down her throat. "Daphne, what is this?"

"Bourbon."

"You think you should be drinking a half hour before the audition?"

Daphne took the glass back from her. "Oh, don't be so uptight. Have you ever known me not to hold my liquor?"

"As a matter of fact—"

Daphne laughed. "Admit it, no one can tell when I've been drinking. Besides, all I've had tonight are a few sips to wet my whistle."

Chapter 3

Susan did not like this at all. She was about to remind Daphne of the times at Briarwood when her drinking had gotten her into trouble, but just then Betty Berke entered the bedroom. Susan stared at her in amazement. Gone were the T-shirt, overalls, and ponytail. Instead, Betty wore a trendy black-and-white Norma Kamali silk dress with padded shoulders. Her orange, curly hair was swept to the side and held with a rhinestone comb. She looked positively sophisticated.

"Betty, you look terrific," Susan exclaimed.

"You do." Even Daphne had to agree.

"Thanks," Betty said brightly. "I do look pretty good."

"Where did you get that dress?" Susan asked.

"I went into Boston and got it at Carpelia," she said, naming an exclusive local boutique. "I thought I needed a new look."

"Well, you certainly got one," Daphne said, still goggling.

"I also got a new song."

"You mean no more 'Beautiful Dreamer'?" Susan asked with surprise.

"Nope. 'Time After Time.' "

Susan shook her head. "Betty, there may be hope for you yet."

After gathering their coats, Susan, Daphne, and Betty hurried out into the nippy spring air and headed toward the music building. They didn't have much to say to each other, but as they passed picturesque Hastings Chapel, Betty broke into the old sixties song "Chapel of Love," and Susan harmonized with her. Daphne didn't sing along, but she didn't put them down either. Susan felt this was a positive sign. If only she'd stop being so hard on everybody.

The music building was one of the newest buildings on campus. Compared to the typical architecture at Hastings, which was old and fussily charming, it had a clean, almost stark look. Definitely an acquired taste, Susan thought, eyeing its cold square entrance.

Betty seemed to agree. "Not very inviting," she said, stopping next to Susan.

"What are we waiting for?" Daphne asked. "Let's go in."

"Right," said Susan, pushing open the doors. "The worst that can happen is they throw tomatoes at us."

Betty giggled, and Susan smiled down at her. Honestly, couldn't Daphne see how sweet Betty was?

She and Betty followed Daphne into the

brightly lit auditorium where the auditions were taking place. A crowd of about twenty girls and several teachers were milling around in front of the stage. Nancy Gurney, the president of the Nightingales was standing near the piano. She was conservatively, almost plainly dressed and her straight brown hair was swept tidily back under a headband. With her above-average height and her big bones, she seemed like an amazon compared to the more compact Jorge. Next to her, Jorge Marquez was looking very *GQ* in black baggy slacks, pink button-down shirt, and pink-and-black Armani sweater. Several of the latest arrivals were waiting in line to greet Nancy and Jorge.

"A receiving line," Daphne noted.

"You mean we have to say hello to him?" Betty gulped.

"Them. Although I don't think it's Nancy you're worried about," said Susan. "What's the difference? You're going to be singing for him in a little while."

"But when I sing for him, he'll be fifty feet away. Now I'm right on top of him."

Daphne looked Jorge over. "Precisely where I'd like to be."

Actually, Susan was not that thrilled about the receiving line herself. Nancy was a big deal in Gamma Gamma Chi and right now the Gammas were the last people she wanted to think about, especially after this afternoon's game of hide-and-seek with the stationery.

That didn't seem to be stopping Daphne, however. She strode unhesitatingly toward Jorge and Nancy.

"Mr. Marquez, I'm Daphne Riesling."

"How do you do?" He spoke with the trace of an accent. "Will you be auditioning tonight as an alto or soprano?"

"Alto," she answered, and he made a notation on his clipboard. "I'm looking forward to singing for you." She put out her hand, which he automatically clasped, but Daphne did not immediately let go. She gave him a wide-eyed look and asked, "Will there be private critiques?"

Politely, he disengaged himself. "Sorry, Miss Riesling, we'll be posting notices. This is Nancy Gurney, our president." Almost imperceptibly, he pushed her in Nancy's direction.

While Daphne and Nancy Gurney made perfunctory small talk, it was Susan's turn to say hello to Jorge. He was gorgeous, no doubt about it. Up close she could appreciate how well his thick curly black hair went with his olive skin. His eyes were a surprising hazel.

"Susan Radcliffe. Soprano," she added.

"Fine. We need sopranos," Jorge said, checking off her name. "What will you be singing tonight, Susan?"

" 'Summertime.' "

"Ah, Gershwin. My favorite." Susan moved off toward Nancy and gave her a quick hello. Then she settled in a front-row seat next to Daphne. She was just in time to see Betty walk up to Jorge and timidly take his hand.

Betty was famous for her blush and this certainly seemed to be the occasion for it. That girl had it bad, Susan thought, suppressing an urge to smile.

"I'm pleased to meet you, I'm Betty Berke," Susan heard her say.

"Nice to meet you, Betty," Jorge answered. "Your song?"

Susan had noticed how Betty's eyes kept slipping away from Jorge's, but now she looked him full in the face. " 'Time After Time,' " she answered, appearing utterly captivated. This time Susan had to smile. Mondo crush time. Poor Betty.

"A lovely choice," Jorge commented. "Good luck, Betty."

As Betty floated off to see Nancy, Daphne leaned over to Susan. "Got some antiseptic?" she mocked. "I do believe Betty's been bit by the love bug."

"Shush," Susan scolded, stifling a laugh as Betty sat down in the seat Susan had been saving for her. Then Jorge got up on the stage and welcomed the crowd.

"I'm happy to see such a large turnout tonight. It shows how many of you appreciate fine music and one of the premier choral groups in the Northeast. Oh, let's just make that the United States."

The crowd laughed appreciatively, but Susan noticed that Betty just sat there, transfixed.

"However," Jorge continued, "the number of aspiring Nightingales is a mixed blessing.

We only have four freshman spots open. That's fewer than usual. The decision, and I'm sure it will be a difficult one, will be made by myself, with advice from Nancy Gurney and the other Nightingale officers. We hope to have the results to you within a week or so. I do thank you all for coming, and now, as they say, on with the show. First up, Margot Williams."

Margot, an attractive black girl who lived at Windsor Hall, mounted the stage, gave her music to the accompanist, and announced her selection, an aria from *La Boheme*. As Margot's rich voice filled the auditorium, Daphne leaned over to Susan and whispered, "I'm thirsty."

"Well, it would be kind of rude to leave," Susan whispered back.

"There's probably a fountain right outside," Daphne replied as she motioned to a nearby door. Grabbing her purse, she scooted out.

When Margot and several other girls had finished and Daphne wasn't back, Susan began to worry. What if they called her? Instead, Susan heard her own name.

Susan's heart fell to her stomach. She loved singing but she was usually part of a group. She wasn't looking forward to stepping out alone in front of a sea of faces. If her imminent solo wasn't bad enough, Susan was distracted by Daphne's disappearance. Trying to put her friend's whereabouts out of her mind, she hurried up the stairs to the stage, smoothing her skirt and nervously running her fingers through her hair. After conferring briefly with the accompanist, Susan stood still for a moment and then launched into "Summertime."

As was often the case with her singing, the music lifted her out of herself. Suddenly, there was nothing but the beauty of each note, and the desire to express perfectly the feeling behind every phrase. Susan felt the piano swell around her and carry her along.

It was only near the end of the number that she noticed Daphne was back in her seat. She was giggling and whispering to Betty, who looked embarrassed. What was going on? Susan turned away with an effort and finished the song to a strong round of applause.

Susan quickly returned to her seat. "Good job," Daphne whispered. Susan's eyes widened in surprise. There was liquor on her breath.

"You idiot, you've been drinking!"

"I couldn't find the fountain, so I had to use my flask," Daphne responded, patting her purse.

"Daphne Riesling," Jorge called from the stage.

Susan watched Daphne slowly walk up to the stage. To the uneducated eye, Daphne looked fine, but Susan had known her far too long not to realize Daphne was tipsy. Then Susan noticed that Daphne's music was lying on her seat. Rather than have to watch

Daphne walk back, she ran over to the stage
with it. Daphne gave her a gracious smile.

"Is she all right?" Betty asked in a concerned voice when Susan returned to her seat.

Susan gave a little sigh. "Don't worry, if
anyone can get through this, it's Daphne."

And she did. Oh, her timing was a little off
in parts, and she really quavered on the last
few notes, but Susan felt it was a perfectly
acceptable rendition of "The Way We Were."

"Pretty good, huh?" Daphne grinned as she
plopped down in her seat.

Susan smiled noncommittally. She turned
toward Betty whose normally high color had
paled to a chalky white. "Are you okay?"

Betty nodded. "I just wish they'd call me."
Instead, they had to listen to five or six more
singers. Betty was the last to be called. She
gave Susan a sick little smile and mounted the
steps as though she were on her way to the
guillotine.

She really did look terrific, Susan thought,
and when she opened her mouth to sing, she
sounded like an angel. Susan had heard Betty
sing before, but she had never sounded this
good. She put every bit of emotion into the
words and looked directly at Jorge while she
sang them.

When Betty finished to quite an ovation,
Jorge came up on the stage and gave her a
dazzling smile. Her face was still turned to
him as she moved down the stairs.

"Thank you all for coming. My decision is

going to be even harder than I thought, but I will have it to you just as soon as possible. Good night and good luck."

The crowd began to thin out and move toward the door.

"Betty, way to go," Susan congratulated her as she put on her coat.

"Well, you too. You're going to make it for sure."

"Isn't anyone going to congratulate me?" Daphne asked petulantly.

Betty looked uncomfortable. "Of course. Look, I want to go over and talk to Margot. I'll catch you back at the dorm."

As Betty hurried away, Daphne turned to Susan. "So what did you think?"

"You did fine. Considering."

"I thought I was wonderful," Daphne said exuberantly as they headed for the corridor. She took the flask out of her purse. "Time for a little celebration."

"Put that away," Susan said, horrified.

"Oh loosen up, Radcliffe," Daphne replied, taking a quick chug. "I'm celebrating. I just made Nightingales."

"You're gonna make squat if you don't stow that *right now.*" Susan made a grab for the flask. Instead of pulling it out of Daphne's hand, as she'd intended, Susan knocked it to the floor. Both girls watched as the amber liquid slowly spread across the linoleum. Several people turned around to look at them, and before Susan could find some tissue in her purse to wipe it up, Jorge appeared on the scene. Susan could have cried. What was the matter with Daphne?

"What's going on here?" Jorge asked sternly.

"Nothing," said Susan, finally locating the tissue in her purse.

"Who does that belong to?" he said, pointing at the flask on the floor.

Daphne gave Susan a hard look. Susan knew it meant Daphne wanted her to take the blame. She had done things like this in the past, but not this time. Susan stared stubbornly at the soggy tissues.

Jorge bent down and picked up the silver flask. The initials D.R. were plainly engraved on the side. Silently, he handed the flask to Daphne. "Please take care of your mess," he said, and walked away.

"Whew," said Daphne, grabbing a tissue from Susan's hand and doing a quick mop job. "I thought he might be mad."

"He was mad, Daphne, couldn't you tell?" Susan wanted to shake her.

Still riding high, Daphne threw her arm around Susan's shoulder and walked her out the door. "Jorge mad at his next star soloist? Don't be silly."

Chapter 4

Susan liked to sleep as late as possible and often missed breakfast altogether. This morning, though, she was too restless to sleep. She kept seeing that tight, cold look on Jorge's face as he handed Daphne her flask. Probably, the incident had queered both their chances of making the Nightingales. And what about Daphne herself? Susan had always taken Daphne's occasional drinking bouts for granted. They were just part of who Daphne was—rebellious high spirits. But now, there really seemed to be something dark about Daphne's drinking, something that wasn't happy at all. Unfortunately, Susan knew Daphne would bite her head off for even suggesting something might be wrong.

Jeez, Susan thought, what kind of friendship have we got if I have to be afraid of mentioning anything sensitive? Then she thought, If I'm not friends with Daphne, who am I friends with? Nobody, that's who.

With thoughts like that, who needed to sleep? By 6:00 A.M. Susan was wide-awake and out of bed. By seven, she was wearing her oldest jeans and sweatshirt, no makeup, her glasses, a ratty old ski jacket, and heading toward the cafeteria. She gave a great yawn and then stopped short because someone was blocking her way. Bruce Shetland. Susan squinted blearily at his crooked eyebrows and his crooked nose and at his annoyingly lively crooked grin.

"My, my, if it isn't Sleeping Beauty," he crooned.

Susan rolled her eyes. It was much too early to be talking to Bruce Shetland.

"I'm hardly a beauty," she snapped, trying to move around his tall, lanky figure.

"Uh-oh, someone got out on the wrong side of the bed this morning. Not me, of course. I'm always the soul of wit and charm from the moment I open my big brown eyes."

Susan just gave in and laughed. There was certainly something engaging about Bruce, if you could overlook his crooked face. The nose especially killed Susan, so patrician—until you noticed that hockey player's bump right smack in the middle. And Bruce's clothes were always mismatched. Today he was wearing traditional cords and a pullover, but with no shirt underneath. The outfit was topped by an authentic World War II leather flight jacket and a long white silk scarf, its tassels blowing in the breeze. When you put everything together, however, it made an attractive and appealing package.

"I'm cold," Susan said, stamping her feet.

"Well, allow me to escort you to our destination. By the way, what is our destination?"

"The cafeteria."

Bruce nodded sagely. "Ah, the barf barn."

"The building that Pepto-Bismol built," Susan agreed.

"Tomorrow we'll go someplace where they don't serve indigestion for dessert," he said as they walked along.

"Why are those three words in the same sentence?" Susan asked coolly.

"Indigestion for dessert?"

"Tomorrow we'll go."

Bruce gave a mock frown. "You mean we're not set for tomorrow night? I thought it was a date."

Susan felt herself weakening. "All right, I have nothing else on."

"Nothing under that attractive outfit?" he said with a little leer.

She gave him a haughty look. "You're disgusting."

"I am," he cheerfully agreed. "But I'll try to plan something nice for tomorrow anyway." They stopped in front of the cafeteria. "There you are, safely delivered."

"You aren't coming in?"

"No, I have to go blow up the chem lab now, but if I don't talk to you, I'll pick you up around eight." He gave her a little peck on the cheek and walked away, leaving Susan shaking her head.

He's crazy, she thought as she headed into the warm cafeteria, but in a fun way. She decided she would go out with him. No matter what they wound up doing, it had to beat sitting in the Windsor Hall lounge watching TV with Daphne.

Susan walked through the crowded dining area to the steam tables. There, bacon, eggs, toast, hot cereal, and pancakes languished in individual silver trays. The bacon looked burnt and the eggs were runny, so she grabbed a small box of cornflakes and put them on her tray. It seemed like she always ended up with cornflakes.

"Any milk?" Susan said shortly to Cynthia Woyzek, a Windsor Hall scholarship student who helped support herself by working in the cafeteria.

" 'Good morning' to you too. There's some over there." Cynthia motioned to a metal pan with melted ice cubes, in which two cartons of milk were floating.

"They look warm."

"But do they taste warm?"

"Cynthia, could you just get me some cold milk out of the refrigerator?"

"Certainly, Susan. I'd hate for you to ruin your cornflakes with some nasty old warm milk."

While she disappeared into the back, Susan tapped her foot impatiently. Wasn't this what Cynthia was paid for?

"Here you are, Susan," Cynthia said, handing her a small milk carton. "Don't drink it too fast, you'll get a tummy ache."

"Oh heck—" Susan started, wanting to explain that she hadn't meant anything by her request. Cynthia shouldn't expect people to be nice at this hour. Cynthia gave Susan *such* a look, though, raising her eyebrows and pursing her lips, that Susan thought better of her good intentions. Mumbling to herself, she turned on her heel and headed into the main room. By now the place was totally filled with students. Susan wandered up and down aisles but couldn't find an empty chair anywhere. When she finally spotted one in the corner and raced over to it, she found herself face-to-face with Cathy Thomas.

Damn, Susan cursed silently. Every time she saw Cathy, she remembered guiltily that she'd forged a love note from Cathy to one of the Phi Delts and put it up on his fraternity bulletin board last fall. That's why Rachel had organized the silent treatment, in defense of her friend. Even though Cathy had accepted her apology, Susan still got embarrassed every time she had to run into her.

Susan was about to turn away when Cathy said, "You can sit down, Susan."

Susan gave a quick look around, but every seat was still occupied. "Thanks," she said curtly, and sat down.

"You're not usually here this early, are you?" Cathy asked conversationally.

"Nope," said Susan, pouring her milk on her cornflakes. She tried to think of something else to say. "Are you always here this early?"

"I get up every morning and run."

"Oh that's right. You're on the track team."

"Have you ever thought of running?"

"Me?" Susan laughed.

"Sure, you've got the right figure for it—slim, long legs. You'd probably make a good runner."

"No, thanks. Too sweaty for me." Susan knew she sounded like a bitch. In fact, bitchiness was fast becoming her natural emotional state. She was going to have to keep an eye on that. Cathy had always been okay to her, even after the stunt she pulled. It couldn't hurt to make a little effort, could it? "So, have you got any races coming up?" she asked.

"Yep. Our track team is going to run against B.U."

To Susan's surprise, she and Cathy spent the next half hour talking about B.U., the merits of Radcliffe versus Hastings, and comparing notes on their lit course.

"Well, I gotta go," Cathy said, gathering her things together. "Good talking to you."

"Yeah, good talking to you," Susan agreed. She knew she was smiling like a maniac, but she couldn't help herself.

Boy, first Rachel, now Cathy Thomas. What was the world coming to? She and Daphne had done nothing but trash those girls all year long and it turned out they weren't half bad.

Susan grinned at the limp remains of her cornflakes. Daphne was going to throw a fit.

It was late afternoon by the time Susan dragged herself back to Windsor Hall. Taped to the door of her suite was a note: *Where are you, Susan? See me as soon as you get in. D.*

Susan sighed and let herself in. What was it this time, she wondered. She went to her room and dropped her books on the bed. Taped to her dresser mirror was another note. This one was from Rachel. "Your stepmother called. Please call her back at the Ritz-Carleton." Scribbled along the bottom was a phone number.

Gloria in town? Gloria hadn't said anything about a trip the last time she'd called. I hope nothing's wrong, Susan thought as she hurried out of the suite to the hall telephone.

Fortunately, it was free. Susan dialed quickly and when the Ritz operator answered, she asked for the Radcliffe suite.

"Hello," Gloria answered in her precisely enunciated upper-class voice.

"Gloria, it's Susan."

The voice warmed up a bit. "Susan, dear. Lovely to talk to you."

"What are you doing in Boston? Is anything wrong?"

Gloria's lilting laugh trilled over the wire. "Of course not. The national board of Children's House just decided to have a meeting, so I flew in. I'll be here tonight and tomorrow." Gloria was on the board of many charities and foundations. Helping others, she often said, was her life's work.

"That's great," Susan said. "So we'll get together."

"Well, I hope so dear. Of course, I'm booked tonight what with the foundation cocktail party, and then there's the meeting all day tomorrow—"

"You sound busy," Susan said, a little wistfully.

"Always, honey, you know that. But I can fit you in for breakfast or an early dinner."

"Breakfast, I guess. I have a date tomorrow night." Susan could have bitten her tongue. She certainly didn't want to tell Gloria about Bruce Shetland.

"How nice, dear. With whom?"

"I'll tell you tomorrow. Shall I meet you at the hotel?"

"Yes, the penthouse suite. And bring Daphne with you, all right?"

"Sure. See you tomorrow."

"*Ciao*, darling."

Susan slowly hung up the phone and walked back to her room. She could never quite sort out her feelings for Gloria, even after all this time. Susan remembered how awful it had been when her mother died. It was just like someone had turned off all the lights and left her alone in the dark. Her father was there, of course, but he was lost in his own grief.

Then, about a year later, Gloria had appeared on the scene. She was tall and blond, sort of like her mother, but she had reminded Susan of frost on a window. Pretty, but nothing you wanted to touch. It was obvious, even to an eight-year-old, that Gloria was going to be a very important part of her father's life. Susan always tried to be good and sweet when she was around, but for some reason, that didn't impress Gloria at all. Susan lived in mortal fear that she would be sent to that most dreaded of places, a boarding school.

Happily, things changed for the better when, shortly after the marriage, the Rieslings moved to Lake Forest. Gloria adored Jean Riesling and she adored her daughter Daphne. Susan quickly realized that if she wanted Gloria to like her, she had to be as much like Daphne as possible. It had worked shockingly well.

Instead of going back to her room, Susan walked down the hall to Daphne's, and since the door was ajar, she went right in. Daphne almost jumped when she noticed her.

"God, you scared me. Where have you been?" she demanded.

"To class, Daphne. Remember? I go to college here."

"Very funny," Daphne replied, sitting back down on the floor near the coffee table.

"I just spoke to Gloria."

"Yeah? How is she?"

"She's here in Boston," Susan answered, flopping down on a couch identical to the couch in her suite. "She wants to take us to breakfast."

"Breakfast? Can't we get dinner out of her?"

Susan chewed on a fingernail. "Well, she did ask, but actually I have other plans for dinner."

Daphne stared at her in disbelief. "What other plans?"

"I'm going out to dinner with Bruce."

"Oh no." Daphne clapped her hand to her head. "I thought we decided—"

"He trapped me," Susan said in a rush. "I just couldn't get out of it."

"And what am I supposed to do while you're gone?" Daphne asked.

"I don't know," Susan said miserably. No one could make her feel guilty the way Daphne could. But why *should* she feel guilty? Oh damn, it was just so hard to stand up to Daphne when she was right there in front of her.

Daphne walked over to her purse and took out a bottle of aspirin. "I've had a headache all day, and you're making it worse," she said accusingly. She shook two tablets into her hand and downed them with a glass of something that was sitting on the coffee table.

"You should have a headache," Susan said, determined not to let her get off so easily. "After last night."

Daphne gave an unconcerned little laugh. "C'mon Susan, I was hardly drunk. Although I wasn't thrilled when you knocked the flask out of my hand and caused a scene. My God, what got into you?"

"You know it was an accident," Susan pleaded.

"Oh well," Daphne said, "no harm done. After all, I'm sure Jorge has seen alcohol before. He's man of the world."

Susan sighed. Daphne was in her own little world if she couldn't see that Jorge Marquez was ultra-straight. "Listen, Daphne," she began tentatively, "it's not Jorge you should be worried about. It's your drinking."

"What are you talking about, 'my drinking'? Pshaw, I'm a better drinker than anyone I know. You're just being an old stick in the mud. Remember how I drank Skippy Whittaker under the table that night?"

"Sure," Susan reluctantly agreed. "But this time it's getting you into trouble, getting in the way of something you really wanted badly."

"Get this straight," Daphne said, suddenly icy. "If anything got in the way of my making the Nightingales, it was your stupid clumsiness." She stared at Susan, so coldly Susan thought she would shiver. Then Daphne shrugged. "Anyway, I told you it's no sweat. We've both got it made."

"I hope so. Getting into the Nightingales is really important to me. Missing out on Gammas was bad enough. I don't think I could stand not making something else."

Daphne lit up a cigarette. "Yeah, I know what you mean. But I'm telling you it's no sweat. As for Gammas, we're going to fix that too. You haven't forgotten the letter?"

"I didn't forget, Daphne. How could I?" Susan asked wearily. "You've been harping on it for days."

"It just so happens, while you were wasting

your time with Bruce, I decided to make the most of the afternoon."

"I only saw him for a few minutes this morning . . ."

"Long enough to say 'yes' to a date. Anyway, you interrupted me. Since we don't know when Betty's coming back, I decided I'd better get started on the letter, so I made a rough draft."

"Great," Susan said unenthusiastically. "Let's hear it." She almost never yelled at Daphne, but today she was pretty near the breaking point. Keep calm, she told herself. You know yelling doesn't work with Daphne.

"Okay. Listen to this." Daphne opened the book where she'd hidden the letter and began reading.

Dear Andrea and Hastings Gamma Gamma Chis:

I am writing to you on behalf of Susan Radcliffe and Daphne Riesling. I have known these girls and their families for a number of years and I can't recommend them highly enough. Not only are their backgrounds impeccable, both girls are fine, upstanding young women, just the sort we need in Gamma Gamma Chi. I cannot tell you how pleased it would make me to see the Hastings Gamma house induct these two marvelous girls.

                    Yours in sisterhood,
                    Mrs. Gregory Dunbar

"So what do you think?" Daphne asked,

looking extremely pleased with herself. "It's not overt, but the pressure is definitely there."

Not overt? Who was Daphne kidding? Susan decided then and there that somehow she had to make Daphne realize what a terrible idea this was.

"Daphne, I think the letter is fine," she began, trying to sugarcoat the truth.

"I knew you'd like it."

"Let me finish. But I don't think we should send it."

"Why the hell not?"

"I wouldn't steer you wrong, Daphne. Sending it is just going to drag out this whole thing with the Gammas."

"I want to drag it out. I want to watch them squirm."

"Let's forget about them. They don't want us. Even if they decide they have to take us for Mrs. Dunbar's sake, they won't be nice to us. Why should we put ourselves in a situation like that?"

"Because we belong with the Gammas. Where else are we going to find girls like us to be friends with?"

Susan raised her voice. "You're talking in circles. First you want to see them squirm, then you want to be friends with them. Which is it? Make up your mind."

"Both. First I want to see them get all crazy because of the letter, and then I want them to let us into Gamma Gamma Chi."

"Well, I don't." The moment Susan said it,

she realized it was true. "I don't want either one."

"Oh, I suppose you want to spend the rest of your college career hanging out with creeps like Betty Berke."

"For your information, Daphne," said Susan, throwing caution to the winds, "there are some very nice girls in this dorm."

"Yeah, like who?"

"Like Cathy Thomas. Like Rachel Pirnie."

"Rachel?" Daphne looked as though Susan had slapped her and Susan knew she had gone too far. "What about Rachel?"

Backpedaling, Susan said, "It's nothing."

"No," Daphne said, "it's more than nothing."

"Oh, hell. Look, last night she just said we shouldn't fight so much. No big deal."

"So Rachel threw you a crumb. I suppose now you want to stay roommates with her," Daphne said, her voice shaking with anger.

"It's too late in the semester to start changing around," Susan said, trying desperately to sidestep the issue. "We'll just do it next year."

Daphne ran her hand through her wavy hair. "You're just going to stay there with my worst enemy?"

"I'm tired of enemies. Aren't you? That's why I want to forget the letter. It's never going to work and it will only make us more enemies in the end."

Daphne agreed. "You know, you might be right about that." She seemed to have her voice under control now.

"Do you really mean that?" Susan asked, feeling like Daphne had just lifted a great weight off her shoulders. "I'm so glad. I mean, I don't expect you to be best buddies with Rachel. I don't expect to be best buddies with her myself. But honestly, I get so tired of fighting with everybody, and I just figured you must, too, sometimes. I mean, we're big girls now. We have to learn to get along with people who don't, well, meet our high standards." Susan leaned closer to Daphne, trying to coax a smile out of her. Daphne just stared at the glowing tip of her cigarette.

"And maybe we could talk about, uh, about why you've been drinking so much lately," she added unsurely.

Daphne looked displeased. "Sure," she said distantly. "Sometime." She rubbed her forehead. "But for right now, I just want to shake this damn headache. I think I'm going to lie down for a while."

Susan gave her an uncertain look. "All right, I've got a lot of studying to do tonight anyway. I'll pick you up for breakfast, I guess."

"Fine," said Daphne, and without another glance in Susan's direction, she picked up the book with the letter in it and headed toward her bedroom.

Susan watched the door shut behind her. She tried to separate the emotions she was feeling: anger, upset, worry that she had pushed Daphne away instead of pulling her closer. There was a time not too long ago, when she and Daphne always seemed to be on the same wavelength. How could this have happened to a friendship that had once been so close? It made Susan feel very alone. Surprisingly, the feeling wasn't a hundred percent unpleasant.

Daphne sat at her desk, eyes swimming with furious tears. Self-righteous, sneaky little traitor—making friends with Rachel behind her back, when she knew darn well it would drive Daphne crazy. And then mumbling all that smarmy stuff about "her drinking." Susan should know better. Obviously the girl needed to be taught a lesson about what happened to people who betrayed their best friends. Their only friends.

Daphne slid the Dunbar letter closer. Susan did have a point about one thing. This letter definitely could cause problems for someone. Slowly, Daphne took up her pencil. She smiled as she made a few choice corrections in her rough draft, calm now that she was acting on a plan.

Susan would come crawling back by the time Daphne sewed up this little scheme. She would have to, because she wouldn't have another friend in the world.

Betty Berke returned to the suite an hour later. She called Daphne's name, but no one was around. Just as well, Betty thought. Now Daphne couldn't argue about giving back her

Norton Anthology. Daphne had borrowed the book a week ago after she'd misplaced her copy. Well, she could just buy a new one, Betty thought, looking around for it.

Finally, Betty found it on Daphne's desk. As she was reaching for the anthology, she noticed a letter written on expensive-looking Gamma Gamma Chi stationery. Surprised, Betty picked it up and began reading.

It was a letter from a Mrs. Gregory Dunbar asking the Gammas to pledge Susan Radcliffe. That was strange. The Gammas had already turned Susan down. What was the letter doing here? Betty looked at the letter more closely. She was sure it had been written on Daphne's typewriter. She had used the machine often enough to know it always sort of jumped on the letter *T*.

None of this made much sense, but Betty sure wasn't about to ask Daphne or Susan what it meant. If she did, they'd know she'd been reading other people's mail. Carefully, Betty put the letter down, picked up her English text, and walked out the door without a backward glance.

Chapter 5

The next morning, Susan walked slowly down the corridor to Daphne's suite. She had spent another sleepless night agonizing over her fight with Daphne.

Susan felt pretty terrible about it. Daphne was her best friend, she always had been, and she always would be. Even if Daphne could be obnoxious and suffocating, Susan told herself firmly, she could also be witty and fun. She could make Susan feel like a privileged member in a very exclusive club. Somehow, she had to make Daphne see reason. These vindictive obsessions of hers were ruining her life. Susan didn't kid herself that last night's talk had done the trick. It would be a long trek, and Susan didn't have an inkling of how to begin. Susan took a deep breath and knocked on Daphne's door.

Daphne was all smiles when she answered. "C'mon in. I'll be ready in a sec."

"Oh, okay." Susan was surprised. This was hardly the reception she'd been expecting, but it had to be a good sign.

"Hi Susan," Betty called from the couch as

Daphne disappeared back into the bedroom.

"What's up?" Susan settled into a chair to wait for Daphne.

"Not much. You look very nice."

Susan was wearing the kind of outfit she knew Gloria loved: an elegant wool sheath, pearls, and high heels. "Thanks. We're going to Boston to see my stepmother."

"That's nice. I don't know what I'm going to do. Cathy Thomas and I were talking about going into Cambridge, but I might stop over at Jorge's house to see if he has the results of the audition yet."

"Jorge?" Susan raised her eyebrows.

"Oh, I don't call him that," she said with a nervous giggle. "Not to his face."

"Have you ever been to his house before?"

"We-ell, no."

Susan wondered if she should be the one to break the news to Betty. Oh heck, she liked Betty, and the idea of letting her embarrass herself sort of made Susan squirm.

"I'm not sure Jorge would appreciate your dropping over," she said carefully.

"You don't think so?"

"He'd probably consider it pressure."

Betty sighed. "Yeah. I don't guess I would have had the guts to go anyway. But isn't he wonderful, Susan?"

Wow, did this one have it bad. "We're talking awesome, Betty, no doubt about it."

"I knew you'd understand." Betty smiled gratefully. "After all, you saw him in action too."

"You getting some action, Betty?" Daphne said, entering the room. "I thought you'd been on the straight and narrow since you broke up with Mitch."

Betty didn't answer, so Susan broke courageously into the gaping silence. "We have to be at the hotel by ten. Let's hustle."

"We're out of here." Daphne smoothed out her suit and found her purse. " 'Bye Betty. Be careful out there."

The moment the girls were out of Windsor Hall, Susan brought up the topic of last night's fight. "Daphne, I think we should talk about it. Clear the air."

"I don't," Daphne said as she hurried toward the bus stop. "It's over, it's a bore."

"Look, I know you're upset about Rachel, but you really have no reason to be. It's not like she's replacing you," Susan said.

"Oh really?" Daphne stared at her with an expression Susan couldn't quite read.

"She simply told me she was tired of living in an armed camp. I agree."

Daphne brushed this aside. "Sure, forget about it."

"And about the Nightingale audition . . ."

"Quit apologizing already," Daphne snapped, unaware that Susan was trying to bring up her drinking problem. "I told you, Susan, I don't think Jorge seeing that bottle will make a difference. And if it makes you feel any better, I admit that worrying about the Nightingales has put me on edge. It's time

Mums found out she's not the only talented one in the family."

Susan was surprised at the intensity of Daphne's statement. But before she could say anything else, the bus pulled up and the girls had to run to the corner to catch it. Daphne began telling Susan the latest campus gossip and she soon had Susan almost choking with laughter. To Daphne, being mean and being funny were synonymous. Daphne was very mean and very funny.

By the time they reached the Ritz-Carleton, Susan felt they were almost back on their old footing. This would make the breakfast with Gloria a lot easier. Her stepmother would be very upset if she thought they were fighting.

The bus let them off near the Ritz in the heart of Boston. The hotel had a quiet grandeur from the outside, and the lobby was beautifully appointed. Susan knew the penthouse suite in which her parents always stayed had one of Boston's most breathtaking views.

As soon as they stepped off the elevator, Gloria flung open the door and ushered them inside. The magnificent suite was all warm woods and bright yellows. It was cheery even on the coldest winter day, and when the sun was shining, as it was now, it positively glowed.

"Susan, dear." Gloria bussed her cheek. "And my beautiful, Daphne," she exclaimed, kissing her too. "It's wonderful to see you both." She put her arms around each girl's waist and led them over to the couch.

"How are you, Gloria?" Susan asked. "And how's Daddy?"

"Fine, fine. Your mother sends her love, Daphne."

"You look wonderful, Gloria," Daphne said. Susan noticed both Daphne and her step-mother were wearing the same color of pink.

"So, darlings, tell me all the news."

"Oh, there's not much happening," Susan said.

"Have you heard anything from the Gammas yet?"

Susan looked at Daphne, who gave a slight shrug.

"Actually, we have. We didn't make it."

Gloria looked stricken. "Didn't make it? Neither one of you?"

"Nope," Daphne said.

"How awful. What could those silly girls have been thinking of?"

"Gloria," Daphne shook her head. "I asked myself the exact same thing."

"Of course neither your mother nor I went to colleges where they had sororities, so you couldn't be legacy, but, naturally, I assumed with your backgrounds and position . . ."

Fortunately, Gloria's thought was cut off by the formally dressed waiter wheeling in breakfast. In the confusion of moving to the linen-covered table and being served their croissants, eggs, and coffee, the subject of Gamma Gamma Chi was misplaced. Susan heartily hoped it would stay that way. Talk moved to Lake Forest and people they knew at home. Susan had almost decided it was safe to breathe when, just as they were finishing up, the conversation turned to her upcoming date.

"Now, I want to hear all about this young man you're seeing tonight," Gloria said, dabbing her lips daintily with her napkin.

Susan groaned inwardly. Here we go. "There's nothing to tell," she said, pasting a smile on her face. "He's just a guy."

"And does this guy have a name?"

"Bruce Shetland."

"Shetland. I know a Lacey Shetland in Chicago. Lovely family. She's president of the Junior League, I believe. Perhaps they are related."

"I don't think so, Gloria," Susan said, twisting her napkin, her eyes down.

"Well, you certainly won't know unless you ask him, will she, Daphne?"

"Oh, I'm sure Susan already knows, Gloria. You can tell by looking at Bruce he doesn't have those kinds of connections."

Susan jerked her head up. Bruce's social status—or lack of it—was the last thing she wanted Gloria to know.

"But who cares if he's not *Social Register*?" Daphne continued amiably. "I'm sure he must be nice if Susan likes him."

Gloria shot Susan the "I'm disappointed in you" look Susan had hated since grade school. "Really, Susan, your father and I are hardly sending you to college to waste time on boys who aren't of our class. Of course, I expected you to meet young men of all backgrounds, but do you really think you want to go out with them?"

"I'm sure it will only be one date," Susan mumbled.

"See that it is, dear," said Gloria coolly as she touched a manicured hand to her hair. "Well, I hate to cut this short, girls, but I do have a board meeting to attend."

"How's your charity work coming?" Daphne asked politely as they all got up and left the table.

"Fine, fine. You know, of course, that charity work is my life, but frankly, it doesn't seem as gratifying to me as it once did."

"No?" Daphne said as she put on her coat. "Why is that?"

"I'm not sure, Daphne. Of course the children's charities like Children's House are lovely, but the adults we see are different. At the women's shelter in Chicago, for instance. I'm the rummage chairperson and we collected all sorts of nice things this year and the women in the shelter didn't even seem grateful. Why, they almost seemed to resent me."

Daphne shook her head sympathetically, though Susan couldn't tell if she was taking Gloria seriously or not. As they said their good-byes, Gloria handed Susan a twenty-dollar bill. "Take a cab, darling, I can't stand the idea of you in a bus."

As soon as they were out the door and into the elevator, Susan lit into Daphne. "So you thought you could get back at me by mentioning Bruce."

Daphne looked at her as if she were out of her mind.

"What are you talking about?"

"You had to mention Bruce has no social connections?"

"Susan, you've got it all wrong. I was sticking up for you. You *heard* me say I didn't care about him not being *Social Register*. You heard me say he was probably nice."

Susan thought about this as they walked through the lobby. That is what Daphne had said; maybe she had just misunderstood her intentions. "Well, you just shouldn't have said anything," Susan muttered. "You know how Gloria is."

Daphne squeezed her arm sympathetically. "Yeah, I do know. Guess I just wasn't thinking."

Susan didn't want to continue the conversation in front of the doorman or the cabbie, so the ride home was very quiet. As soon as they walked into Windsor Hall, however, Agatha Mitchell, the tall Texan with the heavy drawl, yelled down the hall to Susan, "Sugar, this is your lucky day."

"Why's that?" Susan asked curiously.

"Randy Applewood has phoned here at least three times looking for you."

Randy Applewood! Susan's heart started beating a little faster as she pictured his husky good looks. Don't get your hopes up, girl, she told herself. He probably just wants to borrow your chem notes. Still, she made a beeline for the telephone.

When she reached Randy at Chi Eps, she found he had something far more interesting than classwork on his mind.

"Susan, the guys are throwing a small bash tonight. Nothing humongous, just a quiet little get-together. Can you make it?"

Bruce Shetland's face flashed in front of her. They were supposed to have their long-awaited date tonight. He would be so disappointed if she canceled. On the other hand, Bruce was bound to ask her out again. Susan knew better than to expect the same tenacity from a hunk like Randy. This could be her one and only chance. "Of course, Randy," she said, suppressing a twinge of guilt. "I'd love to come to your party."

"I'll come by about seven-thirty."

"You've got it. See you then."

Susan practically danced back to her room. Daphne was waiting.

"So, what did he want?"

"A date," Susan said happily. A date with a handsome preppy jock. No one could say Randy Applewood wasn't the "right kind."

"What about Bruce?" Daphne asked.

"I guess I'll just have to call him."

"And tell him what?"

"That I'm sick, of course."

But by seven-thirty, Susan still hadn't been able to reach Bruce.

"What am I going to do?" she moaned to Daphne, who was sitting on her bed.

"Stand him up, I guess."

"I can't do that," Susan said, pacing the floor. She didn't want to wrinkle her gray linen pants.

Daphne continued filing her nails. "Then break the date with Randy."

"I don't want to do that either."

"Then you're between a rock and a hard place—as they say."

Susan stopped her pacing long enough to pick some lint off her tweed blazer. Then she slowly looked over at Daphne. "Daphne, maybe you could tell him? Tell Bruce I'm sick."

"Hey, I don't want to do your dirty work."

"Daphne, please. Pretty please with sugar and cream," she said, just as she had when they were little. "When he buzzes, all you have to do is go down and tell him I have the flu. That's it—she has the flu—four words. It would be easy."

Daphne thought it over. "All right. I guess I can."

Susan threw her arms around her. "Thank you, thank you. You're the best friend in the world."

"Now you're cooking," Daphne said, patting her on the back.

Susan sailed out the door with Randy at exactly seven-thirty. Bruce showed up about five to eight.

When he buzzed, Daphne made him wait a few moments while she ran a comb through her lush waves. She was still wearing the dress she had put on for breakfast at Gloria's. Idly, she wondered if Bruce had planned an appealing evening.

She made her way slowly down the stairs and caught sight of Bruce before he saw her. He was wearing a terrific-looking sport coat and shirt, the effect of which was ruined by his baggy leather pants. And his leather tie.

"Hello, Bruce," Daphne said with a smile. "I'm not sure we've really met. I'm Daphne Riesling, Susan's friend."

Daphne was tall, but Bruce must have been about six-three. He loomed over her. "Where's Susan?" he asked.

"She's sick. She has the flu," Daphne answered, a shade too earnestly. No one in his right mind would have believed her.

"I see," Bruce said slowly. Nothing wrong with his mind, Daphne thought.

"Did you have something special on for to-night?" she asked politely.

"I have nine o'clock reservations at Le Bec Fin."

Le Bec Fin! One of the most beautiful French restaurants in Boston. Four star all the way. "What a disappointment. It's supposed to be just wonderful."

"Yes, it is."

Obviously, Bruce was going to make this hard for her. "I've always wanted to go there."

Bruce gave her a little half smile. "Have you?" There was a long pause. "Then why don't you join me? Seeing as I have the reservation and all."

"Gee." She pretended to think it over. "It doesn't seem right. Leaving Susan alone, I mean."

"I have a feeling she won't mind."

"You're right," Daphne said gaily. "Let me go and get my coat. I'll only be a second."

Chapter 6

Susan snuck another look at her watch. Only ten o'clock. This had to be the world's longest night. Randy hadn't been lying when he said this would be a quiet gathering. Rather like a funeral she had been to once. The Chi Eps were the jocks house on campus. She had expected them to be a little more rowdy. And a little more fun. Instead, they sat around in a kind of daze talking football to each other. Their dates watched.

With her glasses off, Susan could just make out Randy's form across the Chi Eps rec room. He was at the bar getting yet another drink for himself. She was still nursing her second and really didn't want anymore. Even getting drunk couldn't improve this party.

The evening had started promisingly enough. When Randy came to pick her up, her heart had fluttered the way it always did at the sight of his broad shoulders and cool gray eyes. But on the way over there hadn't been much to talk about. She was almost relieved that he'd disappeared as soon as they got to the Chi Eps—until she checked the crowd.

Then she figured she was in for a long night.

"So," she said when he had finally returned. They were scrunched together on a battered love seat. "Heard about those Nightingale tryouts?"

"Mmmm," he said, which could have meant anything.

"They were like totally gruesome," Susan jabbered nervously. "You know, there's only a few spots open this year. Daphne and I—that's my friend, Daphne—are just dying to get in. I don't know what we'll do if we don't."

"Sure you don't want another brewski?" Randy said, his boozy breath in her ear.

"No thanks."

"Well, just you hold on, sugar. We're going to have something here in a few minutes that'll do the trick. They just ran out before we got here."

Susan narrowed her eyes. "Ran out of what?"

"You'll see," he said in a singsong voice as he threw his arm around her shoulder.

"Randy, where's the ladies' powder room?" Susan tried to ask. "I'm not feeling so well. It must be a touch of the flu." But Randy had already staggered off to join yet another endless sports discussion, this one about the World Series chances of the Boston Red Sox. Disgusted, Susan climbed the rec-room stairs and made her way out into the hallway. The corridor was dark and she almost bumped into Rachel Pirnie.

"Rachel," Susan said, startled. "I didn't see you downstairs."

Rachel shook her head. "I'm upstairs with Scott, listening to music in his room. I wouldn't go to a Chi Eps coke party. And frankly, I'm sort of surprised that you would."

Coke! Suddenly everything became clear to Susan. All those people down there were wired. Didn't they know coke could kill?

Well, if they knew, they certainly weren't concerned about it. And what had Randy called it—"doing the trick?"

"I didn't know," Susan admitted. "Not until you told me. I think they were already high by the time Randy and I got here."

"So what are you going to do?" Rachel asked with concern in her voice.

"I'm going to go home. I don't want any part of this scene. Where do you think they stashed my coat?"

But before they could begin looking for it, Randy lumbered up the stairs. "Where you been, sugar?"

"Randy, I told you I'm not feeling well. I think I'd better go home."

He gave her a lopsided grin. "No way, the fun's just about to start." He handed her the beer he was holding. "Here, finish this up. Then I've got something special I want you to try."

Susan gave Rachel a stricken look. "I said I wasn't feeling well."

"Don't worry, we'll make you feel better—fast."

"She said she doesn't want to," Rachel interjected.

"Butt out, Pirnie. Why don't you go back upstairs and find that wimpy boyfriend of yours while me and the lady here have some fun."

Susan tried to push her way past Randy, but he was blocking her. Rachel stomped on his foot. With a howl of pain, Randy moved aside.

"C'mon, let's go to Scott's room," Rachel said.

Before they even reached the stairs, though, Scott had bounded down into the hallway. He looked at Susan's frightened face and saw Randy grasping his toe and howling in pain. Scott didn't ask what was wrong; he just ushered the girls outside.

"Randy wanted to do some coke and Susan didn't go for the idea," Rachel said simply.

"I see."

"I'm going back to Windsor," Susan said. It had been a bad night and the sooner it was over, the better.

"Let us drive you," Rachel said.

"No, I'll be okay."

"Sorry, we insist." Scott directed her toward the car and helped her inside.

Scott and Rachel were both very sympathetic on the way home, but Susan only listened to their conversation with half an ear.

She wondered where Bruce Shetland was right about now.

"Is there anything else I can bring you?" the tuxedoed waiter asked. "More bread, perhaps?"

Daphne shook her head daintily. "I couldn't; I'm so full." Everything had been marvelous. The lobster bisque, the rack of lamb with tiny vegetables, the salad. How very European of them to serve it at the end of the meal. "This is a beautiful place, isn't it?" The tables were small, intimate and all embellished with fragile bouquets and crystal candle holders. The light from the small flames cast a romantic glow on the diners.

Bruce looked around. "Yep, I think Bordino was the designer. The way he uses wood inlays on the floor and on the tables is his trademark."

By now Daphne was not surprised at the extent of Bruce's knowledge. Apparently, he was a guy who knew something about everything. So far he had talked about Shakespeare's first folios, the *Tibetan Book of the Dead*, the heresies that caused schisms in the first-century Church, and the proper way to poach sole. On the lighter side, they had talked about the outcome of the Kentucky Derby and the history of soap operas. Soap operas were the only subject to which Daphne could really contribute. She never missed "All My Children."

Over the course of the evening, Daphne

tried repeatedly to bring up her favorite topic —herself—but without much luck. No matter how much she turned on the charm or looked at him adoringly with her azure eyes, Bruce just kept going off on tangents of his own.

The waiter silently appeared again and handed Bruce the dessert menu. "Our specials tonight are baked Alaska and chocolate peppermint mousse," he said. "I can recommend them both highly."

Bruce handed Daphne the dessert menu. "Anything look appealing to you? The mousse? Or maybe the raspberries and cream?"

Daphne gave a little laugh. "I don't know. Maybe I shouldn't have anything. I have to watch my weight, you know."

Bruce smiled. "Whatever you say. Waiter, make that one mousse. Now, let's see, I was about to tell you about backgammon. It's my favorite game, you know. Very popular in the Roman empire. This is how it's played. . . ."

Chapter 7

"Le Bec Fin," Susan said for about the tenth time. "I don't believe I missed dinner at Le Bec Fin."

Susan and Daphne had decided to give themselves a Sunday treat and have breakfast at the Primrose Diner where they could discuss their evenings in peace.

"The food was simply marvelous," Daphne said as she added some sugar to her coffee. "Easily as good as La Bastille in Chicago."

"While you were eating rack of lamb, I was eating my heart out," Susan moaned. She had given Daphne a blow-by-blow description of her evening, leaving out the part where Rachel and Scott took her home, of course. Things were just getting back to normal and she didn't want to ruin it. Mentioning Rachel would be like waving a red flag in Daphne's face.

Although, come to think of it, Susan wasn't exactly overflowing with affection for Daphne just now. Daphne, apparently, had had a *wonderful* evening. Either that, or she had chosen this starry-eyed date routine to drive

Susan bonkers. How *could* she have had a wonderful time with Bruce? Susan knew he was much too weird for Daphne. She couldn't count the times Daphne had told her how peculiar he was.

"Bruce really knew how to order wine too," Daphne was babbling. "That rosé he chose—exquisite! I couldn't believe how many topics he could speak knowledgeably about."

Susan stole a look at Daphne's glowing face. She certainly seemed sincere. Susan told herself she'd been too suspicious of Daphne lately. Maybe her friend had more taste than she'd given her credit for. After all, hadn't Susan pleaded with Daphne to be more open-minded about people who didn't "meet their standards?"

Susan attacked her pancakes. "Boy, talk about strategic errors. Do you really think he bought the idea I was sick?"

"I don't know for sure." Daphne shrugged. "We really didn't talk about you."

There was a question Susan had been burning to ask. Finally, she decided to casually throw it on the table. "Did he kiss you?" she asked, glancing sidelong at Daphne.

Daphne hesitated. "Just at the door."

Susan shivered. The thought of Daphne and Bruce kissing, even "just at the door" made Susan a little nuts. How could she have been dumb enough to stand him up? All his appealing quirks came rushing back to her. Could she have lost him to Daphne? Susan put down her fork. "Daphne, let me lay it on the line. I think I made a big mistake about Bruce Shetland. How would you feel if I tried to get him to ask me out again."

Daphne considered Susan's request, then said, "Sure, Susan, I'm not married to him. Give it a shot."

"You're sure? I really feel like you have dibs on him now."

"No, honestly, I don't care."

Susan looked at Daphne with real gratitude. Once again she'd thought the worst of her friend and been wrong. "I don't know how to thank you," Susan said.

"No problem, maybe you can return the favor sometime."

"I will, I will. Are we about finished here?" Susan was restless. With all this talk about Bruce, she really wanted to see him now.

Daphne lit up a cigarette. "I'd like some more coffee. Why don't you go ahead, you're obviously in a hurry."

Susan grabbed her books off the table and headed for the door. "I sure am."

When Susan arrived on campus, she wondered where she should look for Bruce first. Hunter Hall was where Bruce lived, she might as well start there. Trees were blossoming all over campus, and as she walked, Susan had a chance to admire the lovely grounds. Maintaining a brisk pace, she passed the man-made lake that flanked the language-arts building. This was a favorite hangout for lovers and Susan cast longing looks at the couples holding hands and stealing kisses while they roamed the romantic spot.

When she passed the lake, Susan was in the lovely old section of Hastings known as Greek Street. All the fraternities and sororities were there. Passing the beautiful Tudor and Colonial buildings, she could not help but think how nice it would have been to live in the Gamma house. Nice, that is, if they had wanted her. Nevertheless, she was glad Daphne had abandoned her letter-writing scheme. There was no way she wanted to be any part of that.

Finally, Susan arrived at Hunter Hall. The yellow brick building was a male dorm, one of the plainer dorms on campus. Taking a deep breath, Susan marched inside. A chubby boy with glasses was standing at the front desk, reading a book.

"Could you buzz Bruce Shetland's room, please?" Susan asked.

The boy barely looked up. "Bruce went out about an hour ago," he said lazily.

Damn, thought Susan. Now what? Should she leave him a note? What if he didn't answer it? Susan asked for a piece of paper, which the boy gave her. She took a pen out of her purse and began writing *Dear Bruce, I . . .* I what? she wondered. I want you to take me out? She crumpled up the paper and threw it away. Without a word she walked out the door.

Susan decided to try her luck at the student union, but when she arrived it was virtually empty. As she passed the music building, she heard her name being called. Betty Berke was on the steps, looking for all the world like a kid waiting for someone to come out and play. Susan sat down beside her.

"What are you doing here, Betty?"

"Oh, I wanted to see if Jorge had posted the Nightingale list yet."

"They'll be posting it in Windsor Hall too. I think you just wanted to see Jorge."

"Well, neither one of them is here." Betty caught sight of someone coming down the street. "Oh God, there he is." She quickly averted her head, but in a moment Jorge was standing next to them.

"Betty. And Susan, isn't it? Are you waiting for me?"

Betty looked as if she were trying to memorize the cracks in the concrete. Susan realized she was going to have to rescue her. "Just checking on the Nightingale list," she said lightly.

Jorge ran a hand through his thick dark hair. "I'm sorry it's taking so long. I promise I'll have it in a day or so."

"We're not rushing you or anything," Susan quickly interjected.

"Oh, I know. It's just a more difficult decision than even I thought it would be. Say, it's lucky for me you're here. That is, if you have a little time."

"Do you need some help?" Susan asked, as Betty was still mute.

"Yes. I'm trying to get some music

catalogued and the grad student who was supposed to help me is sick today. Would one or both of you be able to help? It really wouldn't take long."

Betty gave Susan a pleading glance, but Susan couldn't tell if it meant please stay or please get out of here. She suspected the former—Betty did have *some* sense. Just now, though, Susan had more pressing business to attend to. Business with a *B* as in "Bruce."

"Gee, I'm sorry, I've got to go," she said, "but maybe Betty can stay."

Tongue-tied, Betty just nodded. Then she managed to squeak out one word. "Sure."

Susan got up and brushed off her pants. "So, I'll see you later, Betty. 'Bye, Mr. Marquez." Then, after one worried backward glance, Susan resumed her search.

She had almost given up hope when she spotted Bruce going into the library. Quickly, she raced up the stone steps and followed him into the building, but once she was at the circulation desk she couldn't see which way he had gone.

Following a hunch, Susan finagled a pass from the librarian and made her way up the circular wrought-iron steps that led to the rare-book room. Sure enough, sitting on a little round step stool was Bruce Shetland.

She walked by him slowly, hoping he would notice her, but he never looked up. Finally, she just went up to him. "Hi, fancy seeing you here."

"Well, if it isn't Sick Susan. Feeling better, I trust."

"Yes, I am. Bruce, I want to tell you I feel just awful about last night." There was an awkward pause while Bruce waited for her to say something else. "At least you had a good time with Daphne."

"Did she tell you that?"

"Of course." Susan looked at him blankly. "*Didn't* you have a good time?"

"Totally rad," he said in a goofy Valley boy voice.

"She said you had a lot in common."

"Let's see, we did share the rack of lamb. Was that it? No, we both watch 'All My Children.' "

"Well, Daphne had a good time," Susan said uncomfortably.

"I'm sure she did."

There was a long moment of silence. Finally, Susan jumped in to fill it. "So what are you doing up here?"

He held out a worn copy of a book. It had crumbling pages and a faded cover that said *Backgammon*. "There's always more to learn about the game of kings."

Susan got excited. "I love backgammon. Maybe we could play sometime."

"Maybe," he said noncommittally. "What are you doing up here?"

She had prepared that answer. "Some history research."

"That sounds vague. Sure you weren't looking for me?"

Her face flushed as quickly as Betty Berke's would have. "No. Why would you say that?"

"I dunno. I thought pancakes were the only kind of stacks you were interested in."

"Pancakes?"

"I saw you at the Primrose Diner. You certainly had a hearty appetite for someone with the flu."

This conversation was not going the way Susan had hoped. "It was only a twenty-four-hour thing."

"That was lucky."

"Yes," Susan hurried on, "well, the thing is, I was hoping we could take a rain check on our date."

Bruce gave her a small smile she couldn't quite read. "Oh, you would, would you? For Le Bec Fin?"

"Well, that would be nice of course . . ."

"Of course."

"But anywhere you say would be fine."

"Good of you. And when shall we make this date?"

Her embarrassment was fading and anger was beginning to take its place. "The twelfth of never, how does that sound?"

Bruce cracked up. "Touché. Let's not wait that long, though. How about tomorrow night?"

That was more like it. "Tomorrow night would be fine."

"This time I'll call before I pick you up."

"Okay," she agreed, slightly ashamed.

"And my motto: no one but Susan. Accept no substitutes."

Susan had to laugh. "I'll be there. So I guess I'll be going now." She turned to go down the stairs. Maybe Bruce wanted to walk home with her, she thought. But when she looked back at him, his head was buried in his backgammon book. He didn't even seem to know she was gone.

Chapter 8

Nothing, Susan thought, I have nothing to wear.

"Clothes problems?" Rachel asked. She came into the bedroom and dumped her books on the bed.

"You scared me," Susan responded in an irritated voice. Then she remembered how nice Rachel had been to her Saturday night and she was ashamed of herself. "Sorry, I'm just nervous about this date with Bruce Shetland."

"Bruce? I didn't know you were going out with him. He's one of my favorite people."

"He is?" Susan was surprised. She had thought Bruce was too strange for most people.

"He's my lab partner in chemistry. I think he's hysterical, don't you?"

Susan smiled. "Sometimes."

"And under that flip exterior, I think he's really very sweet and sentimental."

"Oh, I don't know that he's 'sweet,' " Susan said, turning back to her closet, "but he can be a lot of fun."

"You go for all that society stuff, don't you?" Rachel asked conversationally. "Well, his family is D.A.R. all the way."

Susan just stared at her roommate. Daughters of the American Revolution? How extremely and totally weird. Bruce Shetland was "her kind" after all. To say nothing of Gloria's!

"Why don't we look through my closet and see what's there?" Rachel offered kindly. "It's always more fun to wear something new on a first date."

An hour later, Susan felt like a whole other person. Rachel had dug out a deep purple slit-necked sweater that made her eyes seem almost violet. They paired the sweater with Susan's black pencil-slim skirt and topped the outfit with a pair of dangling silver earrings. Talk about dressed to kill!

Susan admired herself in the closet mirror. "Well, there's not much of me in this outfit, but thanks to you, I look seriously irresistible."

"You really do." Rachel smiled at her reflection. Then they both heard Daphne calling from the common room.

"Susan, where are you?"

"Here I am." Susan turned away from the mirror while Rachel grabbed a book and whispered, "I'm going down to the study room."

"No, stay." Rachel shouldn't be kicked out of her own room just because Daphne was coming.

"That's okay. Catch you later. Have a good

time." She barely looked at Daphne as their paths crossed at the door.

"Hello, Rachel. Good-bye, Rachel," Daphne muttered.

Susan was dismayed to see that Daphne had been drinking again. Yeesh, she had hoped their reconcialiation, not to mention their little talk, had put an end to that. Susan was really getting scared now. "Are you all right?" she asked, concerned.

"Sure. Why wouldn't I be?" Daphne gave Susan an appraising glance. "Hey, you look terrific. Is that a new sweater."

Susan tried to look nonchalant as she turned toward the mirror. She pretended to examine her eye shadow. "Actually, Rachel. loaned it to me," she said, unable to keep a hint of defiance from her voice.

"Is that so?" Daphne exploded. "I'm so glad you and your chum are trading clothes now. What's next? Pajama parties and signing each other's autograph books?"

That did it for Susan. "What is it with you?" she yelled right back. "I'm not allowed to borrow clothes from people without getting your permission? I'm not allowed to speak to anyone you don't approve of?"

Susan could have yelled a good deal longer, but the look on Daphne's face brought her up short. It was so cold, so closed. "What is it?" Susan reached for Daphne's arm, but Daphne flinched away. "Is it that Bruce asked me out again? Were you just being nice when you said you didn't mind?"

"I couldn't care less about Bruce Shetland," Daphne spit out. "And frankly, I couldn't care less about you!"

Susan was shocked by the intense look of anger on Daphne's face.

If looks could kill . . .

"You don't mean that," Susan protested. "You know you don't. Jeez, Daphne, we're buddies—best buddies."

Daphne lifted one skeptical blond eyebrow.

"Daphne! Look, maybe I *haven't* been spending enough time with you lately. Maybe we could plan a big shopping excursion for this weekend, like we used to. How does that sound?"

Daphne shrugged. "Don't rearrange your schedule on my account," she said, as if the whole thing bored her to tears. Nevertheless, Susan noticed she looked a little calmer.

"Hey," she said, in an attempt to lighten things up. "You'll never guess what Pirnie let slip about Shetland's family."

"What's that?"

"Get this—his background is impeccable. His relatives all had staterooms on the *Mayflower.*" Suddenly, Susan was sorry she'd mentioned it. It wasn't like she really cared any more about that *Social Register* stuff. Plus, the news hadn't perked Daphne up any. Susan watched her grit her teeth.

"So he probably is related to that woman Gloria knows," Daphne said tightly.

"I suppose so. I like to died when I heard it. Pretty weird, huh?"

"You bet."

"Listen, I don't want to keep Bruce waiting . . ."

"Of course not."

"So I'm just going to wait down in the lounge."

"Have fun," Daphne said brusquely.

"I will," Susan said. "Don't wait up."

Even though she was a few moments early, Bruce was already waiting when she got downstairs. Susan's heart skipped a beat when she saw him standing near the doorway. He looked so cool in his "Miami Vice" jacket with the sleeves pushed up to the elbows and his pleated pants. Personally, Susan would not have chosen tooled cowboy boots to wear with the outfit, but that was part of Bruce's charm.

The moment he caught sight of Susan, Bruce gave a long wolf whistle. Heads turned up and down the corridor.

"You certainly make your presence known," Susan said as she hustled him out the door.

"I might say the same for you." Bruce steered her in the direction of his car, a Toyota MRZ with a pair of fuzzy dice hanging from the mirror.

"Nice, dice," Susan commented. She was surprised to see Bruce was gentleman enough to help her into the car.

"Hey, let's only talk in rhyme tonight." He buckled his seat belt and indicated that Susan should do the same. "Actually, the dice are a tribute to backgammon. Seeing them swinging there reminds me of some of my past glories."

"I think you may have met your match."

"Is that so?" He moved the car in the direction of the freeway.

"I learned the game at my father's knee. I must have been playing when I was seven or eight."

"Big deal. My mother played backgammon the whole time she was pregnant. When she was sitting at the backgammon table, I could hear her shaking the cubes. I wanted to play so badly, I was two months premature."

Susan grinned. "Yeah, right."

"Well, we certainly must have a match someday."

"Someday soon."

"But we mustn't rush into anything. We have the whole long night ahead of us."

"What time are our reservations?" Susan asked, looking at her watch.

"You know, since it's Monday night, I figured we didn't need reservations. I'm sure it won't be busy."

"You were right, it isn't busy," Susan said as they drove slowly past the entrance to Le Bec Fin. "It's closed."

"Closed on Monday nights," Bruce read, peering out his window at the sign. "Darn. This must be what those ads mean when they say phone first."

Susan gave Bruce a strange look. He seemed mighty cheerful for someone whose plans had just been dashed. She could hear her stomach rumbling. "Now what?" she asked.

"We-ell, the Landing is always nice," he said.

Susan brightened.

"But that's so dull. I'm sure you've been there a hundred times."

"More like once," Susan muttered, but Bruce didn't seem to hear. He was pulling back out into traffic now, hands skimming expertly over the wheel.

"Then there's Rosemary and Thyme—a little more interesting but, frankly, all that vegetarian hoo-ha gives me gas."

Susan rolled her eyes and sagged back in the seat. Suddenly Bruce slapped his palm against his head.

"I'm a genius," he exclaimed. "We'll go to Bruno's."

"Bruno's," she repeated doubtfully.

"Bruno's! The ultimate in Boston restaurants. A dining experience *extraordinaire.*"

Susan couldn't help smiling at his extravagant enthusiasm.

"You are going to love this," he promised. "Real local color. Plain, but exquisitely prepared food. Hearty enough to quiet that grumbling tummy." Bruce nudged Susan's ribs with his elbow. Susan blushed.

"Bruno's," he finished grandly, "is the kind of place only those in the know know."

"All right," Susan laughed. "I'm game."

For some reason this declaration made Bruce pause, but in a moment he was off again, singing the praises of Bruno's, the home of better-than-home cooking.

Susan felt slightly less game when she saw the neighborhood they were driving into. It looked suspiciously like skid row. Oh well, she told herself, I guess that's where you find little places like this. Bruce pulled into the empty curb with a flourish.

"Are you sure this is it?" Susan asked.

He pointed at a neon sign blinking above a dingy cafe. "Bruno's," it said.

"Come on," Bruce coaxed. "Where's your sense of adventure?"

"I don't know, Bruce, it looks pretty crummy."

"Crummy is in the eyes of the beholder, Susan. To me this looks like an oasis in the desert, and it should to you too. That is if you're hungry as you sound."

"All right," she said wearily. "Let's just eat."

"That's my good girl." He helped her out of the car as though he were escorting Cinderella from her carriage. "This is the experience of a lifetime. You've probably never been anywhere like this."

She certainly hadn't. The smell of day-old grease and burnt food hit her nostrils the second she walked in the door. The place was deserted except for two dingy down-and-outers, one of whom was adding muscatel to his coffee. Behind the counter, a heavy-set man in a dirty apron was smoking a cigarette and reading the racing form. Bruce directed her to one of the rickety tables, and Susan sat down shaking her head. She'd skipped lunch for this?

"Bruno," Bruce called as soon as they were settled. "How about a menu?"

The man behind the counter looked up. "I ain't Bruno and the menu's up there." He jerked his head toward a chalkboard that listed three items. Swiss steak, hamburger, and cheeseburger.

"Swiss steak looks like the special tonight, would you like that?"

"No, you were the one who wanted heartier fare, I'll just have a cheeseburger."

"Swiss steak, a cheeseburger, and two Cokes," Bruce called out to the counterman. "And Flower to win in the fifth at Belmont."

"So you know about horse racing?" As miserable as the setting was, Susan decided to make the best of it.

"Among other things. My family owns some horses in Ohio, and I got interested when I started hanging around the stables."

Susan tried to picture him around the stables. Then she tried to picture him at a deb ball. She shook her head. That scenario was just plain ridiculous.

"So-o," Susan said, "what's your family like?"

Bruce froze. "My family? What's my family like? You mean like old money? New money? Money-to-burn money?"

Susan felt her cheeks grow hot. "I *mean*, like mother, father, dogs, and cats?"

"All of the above. And an older brother too. But are you positive you're not interested in our pedigree? I happen to know you've got quite a set of papers yourself. Surely, you must feel entitled to know your date's ranking in the little book of big bluebloods."

"Oh hcck, Bruce, I already know you're one of the Gates Mill, Ohio, Shetlands—"

"Ah-hah!"

"—but obviously you're a heck of a lot more uptight about it than I am."

Bruce fingered his napkin. "Point conceded," he mumbled. "But, really, we're not all that distinguished."

"No?"

"Not since my dad divorced my mom and married the maid. Not since my brother became a Hawaiian beach bum."

"He's a beach bum? For real?"

"We-ell, actually, he's an underwater cinematographer. But he hardly makes any money, honest."

Susan burst out laughing. "You really wish he were a bum, just so you could brag about it. You nasty thing!"

Bruce shook a finger at her. "You, Miss Radcliffe, are much too sharp this evening."

For some inexplicable reason, Bruce's words made Susan glow inside. The moment was broken by a greasy cheeseburger being slapped down in front of her.

"Steak's coming up," the counterman

growled. "So kid, you really know something about Flower?"

"She's a good little filly," Bruce answered. While Bruce and the beefy counterman talked horses, Susan had ample time to consider her cheeseburger. It was not a pretty sight. She wondered idly what horse had provided this gristle. Yuch. She pushed her food away. How could Bruce have been so enthusiastic about this place? Then she had a horrible suspician, so horrible it made her jaw tighten in anger.

"That's good info," the counterman was saying as he walked away. "Now I've got a tip for you. Don't eat the Swiss steak." He looked at Susan. "Or the cheeseburger."

Bruce cocked his head and considered Susan's cheeseburger. "Gee, this place isn't as good as I remembered."

Susan glared at Bruce. Now she was sure. "You knew this place was terrible, didn't you?"

Bruce ignored her question. "Of course, sometimes it's not the food or the atmosphere, it's who you're with. Now say you were here with Randy Applewood . . ."

"I knew it! You planned this whole evening to get back at me. No wonder you weren't surprised when Le Bec Fin was closed. Well, I hope you have a good laugh, Mr. Shetland."

Susan got up and hurried out to the car. Bruce threw a few bills down on the table and followed her. Neither of them said anything for the first few minutes they were in the car.

"Listen," Bruce said, keeping his eyes

firmly on the road. "I can see you're a little ticked—"

"Ticked! *Ticked?* Honey, I'm the whole friggin' clock shop."

"You have to admit—"

"I do not!"

"—you have to admit that what you did to me with Randy Applewood wasn't very nice."

Susan squirmed in her seat until she could face him. "It might not have been nice—"

"What did I tell you!"

"—but it wasn't Chinese water torture, either. You planned this little scene. It was pure, unadulterated, premeditated cruelty."

"Let's not go overboard, here."

"*Overboard!* I'll give you overboard. Overboard is taking a girl to a pest hole in the slums of Boston where she could get mugged or murdered or food-poisoned to death."

Susan was furious to see Bruce's lips twitching with laughter. "Stop smiling, damn you!" She batted him with her purse.

"Whoa, no hitting the driver," Bruce gasped, trying to control himself. "Maybe I did go a little overboard," he admitted after a minute, and for once his voice wasn't teasing or sarcastic. Then he grinned crookedly. "But going overboard is just part of my charm."

"So you say," Susan huffed as they pulled up to Windsor Hall.

She tried to walk to the door without him, but he was out of the car and by her side in a flash. She shook his hand off her elbow.

"Aw gee, Susan," he pleaded. "So I gave you

a bad night. You gave me one too. Now we're even."

"That's your opinion."

"Let's see if I can make it yours too." Suddenly he pulled her close, crossed arms and all, and gave her a surprisingly sweet kiss. Susan fought the urge to kiss him back. "Now are we even?" He smiled as they pulled apart.

"No," she said flatly, and left him goggling as she hurried inside. After what he'd put her through, Bruce had some serious dues to pay.

Chapter 9

Betty spotted a tall, plainly dressed brunette sitting alone in a booth at the far end of the Primrose Diner. Nancy Gurney! Should she walk over and say hello, Betty wondered, or would Nancy find that pushy? Then again, if she didn't say hello and Nancy saw her, Nancy might think Betty was being rude. Certainly, she didn't want to get on the wrong side of the president of the Nightingales.

After weighing all her options carefully, Betty decided to walk slowly toward the booth and let Nancy notice her.

"Oh, hello . . . Betty, is it?" Nancy said when Betty had finally inched over to her table. "Why don't you join me?"

"Oh, gee, thanks," Betty gushed in the breathy way that made her want to kick herself. She had to stop doing that. It sounded so childish.

Nancy's amused smile wasn't making Betty feel too mature, either. "So," the older girl said, her voice full of laughter. "You nervous about the tryouts?"

"Oh no. I mean, well, yes I really am sort of

nervous," Betty finished in a shy little whisper. She cleared her throat and tried to speak up. "There was a lot of tough competition."

"There sure was," Nancy agreed, still grinning. She offered Betty a french fry.

Betty shook her head, barely seeing it. "How—I mean, would it be all right if I asked you, um—"

"How you did at the audition?"

Betty nodded gratefully.

"I don't know if I should tell you," Nancy teased. "I'm really not supposed to discuss it. Seriously, you sounded fine to me. Don't take that as the last word, now," she cautioned when Betty sagged in relief. "Jorge's the one who makes the final decisions. All I do is offer him my opinions."

"Of course." Betty nodded soberly. She felt like a real twit. Thank goodness the waitress had come to take her order.

"Your usual chocolate milkshake?" she asked.

Betty nodded, wishing she could remember the woman's name.

"Those things go straight to my hips," the waitress said.

"Mine too," Nancy moaned. "You're a lucky dog, Betty."

"Fast metabolism," Betty mumbled, wondering how she was going to get through a whole milkshake in front of Nancy. She hoped she wouldn't slurp.

"Nancy," Betty said casually, after the

milkshake had arrived. "He didn't say anything about me? Jorge, I mean?" To Betty's horror, her voice cracked just as she said Jorge's name. And if that wasn't bad enough, her face was flaming now too.

"Oh, Betty," Nancy said, patting her hand. "You've got it too, don't you?" For a minute, Betty thought Nancy meant she had a crush on Jorge as well, but then she said: "Half the girls in the group are mad for Jorge. Don't worry. You'll get over it eventually. They all do."

Betty unconsciously shook her head. That was hard to believe. "I don't really have a crush on him," she said quickly. "It's just, well, he is attractive, you know."

"Sure," Nancy soothed. "Believe me, Betty, when you get to know him, he's just a regular guy."

"He is?" Betty felt her eyes widen. Imagine. Calling Jorge a regular guy.

"Honest," Nancy assured her. "Oh, he flirts, but that's just because he's Spanish. Everybody flirts over there. It doesn't mean a thing. Jorge and I"—here Nancy's eyes misted over —"have a perfect working relationship. It's like he's almost a big brother to me."

"Oh," Betty said, subdued.

"Yes," Nancy repeated. "He's like a big brother."

Susan was about to give Daphne the details of her less-than-wonderful date with Bruce when Betty came bouncing into the suite.

"Hey, Betty," Susan called from her cross-legged position on Betty's bed.

"Am I interrupting anything?" Betty asked timidly.

"Wouldn't stop you if you were," Daphne muttered, avoiding Susan's sharp look. She took a sip of the wine she had poured in spite of Susan's failure to join her.

"Not at all," Susan said, hoping Betty hadn't heard. She patted the blanket next to her. "Come sit down. I'm just about to regale Daphne with the gruesome story of Horror Date Number Twenty-two."

"Uh-oh," Betty said, looking happy as a clam at being included. "It didn't go good with Bruce?"

"The understatement of the year!" Susan roared, and proceeded to spill the whole sordid story.

"Then what happened?" Betty asked, wide-eyed, when she was done.

"Nothing. I came upstairs."

"What a story," Daphne said, drawing out each word.

"It's so romantic," sighed Betty.

Susan couldn't believe what she was hearing. "You think what Bruce pulled was romantic?"

"Sure. Don't you see? He was trying to make you a better person. Kind of like *The Taming of the Shrew*. We're just reading that now in English lit."

"Swell, now I'm a shrew."

"I don't think it's romantic at all," Daphne

said as she sipped her wine. "I think it was creepy. And taking you to that dive. That could have been real trouble." Daphne shook her head. "With his family too. Boy, you can't trust anybody these days."

"So what are you going to do now?" Betty asked.

"I don't know." Susan shrugged. "Got any ideas?"

"You shouldn't see him again." Daphne advised.

"But you're going to run into him," Betty countered. "It's inevitable."

"He's going to call," Susan said thoughtfully. "I'm sure he will."

"Well, I hope you're going to turn him down if he asks you out again." Daphne traced the rim of her wineglass with one long nail.

"Oh, I intend to. But I want to think of some classy way to do it."

"I'm sure if we put our heads together, we can come up with something." Daphne smiled.

Susan wasn't sure how she felt when she woke up the morning after her date—besides stupid and angry, that is. She wondered if it had been like Betty said: Bruce had just been trying to teach her a lesson, to make her a better person. That would still mean he was obnoxious and manipulative, but not cruel. It would mean he still liked her. That he'd be calling again and that Susan would have to decide what to say when he called.

She knew what Daphne would want her to say. They'd both goosed each other to dump bad news boys enough times in high school.

But I'm not sure Bruce *is* bad news, Susan protested silently. Maybe giving him a taste of his own medicine is preferable to dumping him.

Well, she would be able to test her resolve with Daphne today. Daphne had insisted on their meeting between classes to plan strategy. Susan supposed it couldn't hurt. If she was going to buy into this game of one-upsmanship with Bruce, she would need a plan. One thing was sure: Susan didn't intend to let Bruce get the better of her.

When she and Daphne were finally settled with their coffee and Coke at the Student Union, Daphne lit a cigarette and took a long drag. "So, what are you going to do when Bruce calls? We don't want to be caught off guard."

Susan resented that "we" a little, but if anyone could help her think this out clearly it was Daphne. And Daphne would help her defend her pride. Susan had the sneaking suspicion that, without Daphne egging her on, she might just say yes to anything Bruce suggested. "I've been worried about being caught off guard too," Susan confessed, "but the truth is, I haven't come up with a thing."

"Let's practice then. You be Bruce and I'll be you," Daphne suggested. "Now pretend you're calling me."

"Ding-a-ling," Susan trilled.

"Ha-ha, very funny."

"Hello, Susan," Susan said in a voice an octave lower than her own. "It's Bruce."

"Bruce," Daphne said coolly. "I'm surprised you had the nerve to call."

"Why's that, Susan?"

"I didn't think you'd want to remind me of one of the worst nights of my life."

"Hey," Susan said in her regular voice. "Don't you think that's a little rough?"

"No, I want you to be as snarky to him as possible."

"Daphne, I don't want to get rid of him forever, necessarily. I just want to pay him back."

Daphne thought for a moment. "You've got to catch *him* off guard."

Susan considered this. "You're right. He's probably going to expect me to be mad, to avoid him even. So when he calls, I'll act super sweet."

"He'll be surprised," Daphne agreed.

"It'll give him a false sense of security, so he'll feel okay about asking me out. Then when he does, wham, I shut him down."

"And that's the end of Bruce Shetland," Daphne said with satisfaction.

"Well, not exactly, the next time he calls, I'll go out with him."

"If that's the way you want it." Daphne frowned. "Just make sure that when he asks you out the first time, you really give him a hard time."

"Oh, I will. That conversation is going to be

so hot, Mr. Bruce Shetland is going to have second-degree burns on his ear. I can't wait."

But four days later, Susan was still waiting. Bruce hadn't called, he hadn't stopped by. And she hadn't seen him on campus. It was as though he had dropped off the face of the earth.

Thinking about that made it hard to concentrate on Professor Riggs's lit survey course. She stared out the window. Here it was Friday afternoon and instead of savoring her triumph over Bruce, she was still looking for him around every corner. And jumping every time the phone rang. It was getting embarrassing. Susan was always the first one out in the hall whenever it jangled, but it was never for her. If Bruce was trying to keep her off balance, he was certainly making all the right moves.

"And despite the fact that *The Canterbury Tales* was written so many years ago, there are facets of it that speak to all centuries," Professor Riggs droned on.

This was crazy. She was going to flunk out if she didn't start paying attention. She turned her heard firmly toward the professor and concentrated on what he was saying.

"For instance, one of today's most popular games, backgammon, is mentioned in one of the tales. . . ."

Backgammon. Reminders of Bruce even here. Professor Rigg's voice faded as Susan looked out the window. He knows that I'm waiting for him to call, she thought, and every time I wonder about it, I'm playing right into his hands. She sighed as she saw her lovely plan going down the drain. She could hardly turn him down if he wouldn't call her. And she could hardly reconcile with him if she didn't get her revenge first. Trust Bruce Shetland not to cooperate.

It was dusk when Susan left the library. She had gone there after her lit class hoping to get some studying done and it had worked, at least for a while. Since it was Friday night and she had nothing to do, she thought she might go back later on. The library was always pretty quiet on Fridays.

"Susan, can you come with me right now? It's an emergency!" Susan whirled around and saw Bruce looking at her with an excited expression on his face.

All thoughts of playing it cool flew immediately out of her head.

"What is it?" she gasped.

"I'll tell you on the way. Something amazing is about to happen and we have to be there." Without waiting for an answer, Bruce took Susan's hand in a strong grip and pulled her down the stairs.

"Where are we going?" she puffed as Bruce pulled her along.

"Not far," he answered.

It may not have seemed far to Bruce, but Susan thought they were about to make a complete circle of the campus. He was taking her through empty buildings, behind bushes, and down deserted tree-lined lanes. Finally they arrived at their destination.

"Here we are," Bruce said, stopping short.

Susan looked up in amazement. The anthropology building? It was one of the oldest buildings on campus and the most dilapidated. Its crumbling structure and slightly lopsided look made the building seem as ancient as the artifacts it housed.

"Uh-uh," Bruce said, moving her through the doorway. "No time for looking. Not until we get to where we're going."

"Is it somewhere in here?" Susan asked.

"Right here." Bruce led her into a huge anthropology lab. Bones lay everywhere, waiting to be molded in plaster or repaired or identified.

"This is where something amazing is going on?" Susan said, leaning against a counter and trying to catch her breath. "Here in the dinosaurs' graveyard?"

"How do you know these are dinosaurs? Maybe there's a human or two among these bones." He picked up a thigh bone and began spouting *Hamlet*. "Alas, poor Yorick, I knew him, . . ."

Susan laughed. "I believe Hamlet was talking to Yorick's skull."

"He must not have known him as well as I do."

"And he's the emergency?"

"No, actually, the emergency is over here." Bruce took Susan by the shoulder and shuttled her into an office off one side of the lab. In the center of the room, a low-hanging lamp with a green shade hung over a round poker table. On the table lay an expensive backgammon set, all arranged and ready to go. A magnum of champagne had been set to chill in a bucket nearby; red roses, a huge bouquet of them, perfumed the air.

"What is all this?" Susan asked, puzzled.

"When last we saw each other, there was a difference of opinion. I thought my little, uh, fabrication about the restaurant made us even. You didn't. Obviously, there's only one way to settle it, on the backgammon board. Whoever wins the most games is right."

"You're crazy, you know that?"

"*Moi?*"

"Just look at you," Susan said, noticing his outfit for the first time. "You are wearing jeans, a button-down shirt, and a tuxedo jacket."

"I felt the match should be formal. But not too formal."

Susan fleetingly remembered her plan. "I can't stay here."

"Why not?"

"I have other things to do."

"You have a date."

Susan wanted to lie, but she couldn't quite make herself do it. "Not exactly."

"What exactly?"

"I told Daphne I'd have dinner with her."

"I imagine you've already had dinner with Daphne a thousand times too many for one lifetime. Besides, I took the liberty of leaving a messagè for Daphne saying something came up and you'd see her whenever."

"That took some nerve."

"Now, now, none of that nasty Susan stuff. I'm not real fond of that Susan. I like the confused Susan, the one I met wandering around campus last fall. The one who couldn't find her economics class."

Susan's warning lights went on. "And you think that's the real Susan?" she asked.

"Of course."

"Are you sure?"

"Well, if that's not the real Susan, who is?"

Susan smiled evilly. "I think you'll just have to wait and see. Anyway, I didn't come here to discuss my multiple personality. I came here to beat the pants off you."

Bruce leered happily. "Wish you'd try."

"You pervert," Susan laughed. "I'm going to enjoy seeing you grovel."

Bruce rubbed his hands together. "Great, but I'm not really into groveling. Lurking's my bag, watching unsuspecting co-eds from around dark corners."

"Stop, you're sending chills up my spine."

"Can I help it? I love watching pretty co-eds." He pulled a rose out of the vase and handed it to her. "And I like watching them even more when they put roses in their hair. But, careful with the thorns. I'm not real fond of bloody co-eds—no matter how pretty they are."

Susan fiddled with the rose while Bruce

uncorked the champagne and poured each of them a glass. Then he pulled two·battered leather chairs up to the table. "Sit down, sit down."

Susan stuck the rose in her hair. "Are you sure this won't distract you, Mr. Lurker?"

"Nope, it'll make you more fun to beat."

"Sit down and roll the dice, Bruce."

Three hours and five games later, Susan was ahead by five points. "Yippee," she shouted as she took her last chip off the board. "I win, I win."

Bruce mopped his brow. "Wait, who said this match is over?"

"Look, I'm hungry, and I've had too much champagne on an empty stomach. You starved me last time out. I'm not going to let you do it again."

"I thought about food," Bruce said indignantly. "And I don't pull the same trick twice. It just so happens this affair is being catered."

Just then, an elderly man with a mop and bucket in one hand and a white sack in the other came into the room.

"Joe," Bruce greeted him. "Perfect timing."

Joe put the sack on the table, knocking a few chips off in the process. "Things all right in here?"

"Sure. Joe Evans, this is Susan Radcliffe."

"Howdy. This is strictly against the rules, you know. Wouldn't do this for anybody but Bruce here, and I wouldn't do it for him if I didn't owe him a favor."

"I helped him win a bundle at the track," Bruce whispered behind his hand.

"When you leave," Joe finished, "I don't want to know you've been here."

"You got it, buddy."

"And no hanky-panky."

"Scout's honor. Just a good, clean backgammon match."

"Hmmph. You see he sticks to that, little lady."

"I will, Joe," Susan promised, stifling a laugh as he carried his mop and bucket out of the room.

Bruce was already pulling hamburgers and fries out of the McDonald's bag. "Dig in."

"How in the world do you know that guy?"

"Oh, I have lots of friends," he said vaguely.

"I'll bet," Susan said, biting into a hamburger.

"Speaking of friends, Susan, maybe this isn't any of my business, but do you think Daphne is all that good a friend?"

Susan looked at him sharply. "What do you mean?"

Bruce leaned back in his chair and put one foot on the table. "I just have my doubts about her."

"Daphne and I have been friends since we were eight. We have some fights, I guess, but who doesn't?"

"You're sure she doesn't have it in for you?" Bruce persisted.

"Bruce, if you've got something to say about Daphne, you better just say it."

"I don't want to hurt you, but you know she made it real clear to me that you weren't sick Saturday night."

"She said that?" Susan asked with surprise.

"No, she gave me your message, but it was the way she gave it."

Susan shook her head. "That's no proof. She said she was going to tell you I was sick, and she did."

"What exactly do you see in her?"

"Like you said, it's not your business, but she's neat, and funny. Why, everyone who knows us thinks we're exactly alike."

Bruce shook his head. "You're nothing alike, not really, and don't forget you heard it here first."

"Is this your idea of making me a better person?" Susan asked, her voice dripping with scorn.

Bruce looked startled. "Excuse me?"

"You're going to cure my upper-class mentality by getting me to abandon my oldest friend? Jeez, you're as bad as Daphne."

"At least now you admit she's bad."

Susan slammed the table so hard one of the pieces jumped off the board. "I think it's up to me to decide who my friends are. And, frankly, I don't understand how it concerns you."

A muscle jumped in Bruce's jaw. "It concerns me because she's trying to sabotage me in your book."

"Like you're trying to sabotage her with me?" Susan lowered her voice. She wasn't about to discuss Daphne's problems with Bruce, but she wanted to make her position clear. "You just don't know Daphne like I do. And honestly, if you can't trust me to make up my own mind about something like this, I don't know what you want with me in the first place."

Tired of all this sparring, Susan rose to go.

"Wait," Bruce said, touching her arm. "I do trust you."

He winced at her skeptical look.

"All right, I'll *try* to trust you," he amended. "It's your business. I just don't want to see you get hurt. All right, all right, I'll drop it. But you can't leave." He smiled crookedly, pleadingly.

"And why can't I?" Susan fought the pull of his puppy-dog eyes.

"Because you're the one who challenged me to this match. If you quit now, not only are you a loser by default, you're also a wimp."

"Women can't be wimps," Susan said gruffly, but she did let Bruce tug her back into her seat.

Despite Bruce's lopsided grin, Susan could tell he was still disconcerted by their fight— as she was. All through the first stonily quiet games, he kept stealing speculative glances at her, as if he'd seen something he hadn't expected.

That's right, Bruce, Susan thought, you'll find out the real Susan isn't some little lost lamb you can push anywhere you want.

After a few games, though, they were

talking again. Bruce really was nice when he wasn't trying to push her around.

"You know, you really are nice," Bruce said.

"Don't sound so surprised."

"I'll bet you didn't know I broke one of my rules for you." His hands hovered over the dice.

"What rule was that?"

"Never date girls from good families."

Susan stared at him. "I thought you loved dating *Social Register* types."

Bruce laughed, looking pleased that she remembered. "I lied."

"You do that a lot, don't you?"

"Mmm," Bruce hummed evasively. "I guess I'm just afraid they'll be too much like me."

Susan rolled her eyes. "Bruce, old buddy, nobody's that much like you. Nobody." And she gave him a dazzling smile.

The sun was coming up when Susan and Bruce finally had to admit to themselves, and each other, that it was time to call it quits.

"A tie, a lousy tie," Bruce groaned as he got up and stretched.

Susan took her glasses off and rubbed her eyes. "Ten games each. I guess we've both met our match."

"Now how do we figure out who was right Saturday night?"

They looked at each other. "Rematch!" they shouted in unison.

Bruce got serious for a minute. "I've got to

go out of town for the weekend, Susan. My mother hasn't been having an easy time since the divorce, so I said I'd come in for a few days. I'm leaving in a couple of hours."

Susan didn't like to risk losing the momentum of their reconciliation, but she put a brave face on it. "Family stuff. What are you going to do? I hope it won't be too rough for you."

"Look, I'll call you while I'm gone and we'll go out just as soon as I get back."

"I'd like that," Susan said shyly. Suddenly, Susan felt a little light-headed. Here she was, in a room full of bones and hamburger wrappers—looking terrible, she was sure. And standing right next to her was one of the cutest guys she had ever seen, smiling at her with that wonderful crooked grin of his. A second later, he had his arms around her, holding her up.

"Are you going to faint to get out of kissing me?" Bruce asked, smiling down at her.

"I may do both."

"Good, I always wanted a girl who would swoon when I kissed her."

Susan held up her hand. "Remember, we promised Joe we'd be good."

Bruce took the hand she held between them.

"I'll be good," he said, gently kissing her palm.

Susan shivered at the delicious sensation.

"I'll be as good as you like." Then he pulled her tightly to him and gave her a long, hard kiss. No teasing, no fighting, just the strangely sweet feel of his arms around her.

Susan closed her eyes and buried her fingers in his thick, wavy hair. No more game playing now.

Chapter 10

It was a little early in the morning to be wandering the halls of the music building, but that didn't stop Betty Berke. After all, it wasn't like she planned on letting anyone see her. All she would do was peek at the bulletin board to see if maybe, just maybe, the Nightingales list was up. Then she'd go home. She wasn't going to stop by Jorge's office. She wasn't.

Betty checked one bulletin board after another. Nothing. Suddenly she found herself at the board across from Jorge's office. A light was shining behind his frosted-glass door.

He was here early for a Saturday. Maybe he was working on the Nightingale list even as she stood there.

A shadow moved behind the glass. Petrified, Betty spun back to the bulletin board. The door opened. She heard Jorge's quick, dancer-like footsteps cross behind her. Then they stopped.

"Betty?"

Betty took a deep breath and turned around.

"Oh, hi, Mr. Marquez. I didn't expect to see you here on a Saturday."

He was wearing *jeans*. Jeans and a snug black T-shirt. She could see the outline of his muscular chest. Gosh, but he was good-looking.

And now he was smiling at her, hazel eyes flashing.

"*Lo siento*, I am afraid I have not yet finished with the list. If that's what you are looking for."

"No, I was just, uh . . ." Betty blinked desperately at the board. Her eyes snagged on a flyer with a picture of Don Quixote on it. "Just looking for more information about this, uh, Summer in Spain program."

"Ah," Jorge said, moving right next to her. She could smell his after-shave. Aramis. *"Hablas espanol?"*

"Um, a little. *Un poquito.*"

Jorge ruffled her hair. "*Un poquito*, eh? Well, that program is certainly a good way to improve. Since you stay with a real Spanish family, you are constantly surrounded by the language. It is a case of speak Spanish or else." He chuckled. "I may be a faculty adviser for the program myself—if my course proposal is approved."

"Oh," Betty said stupidly, suddenly imagining Jorge on a white Spanish beach, in a bathing suit . . .

"Now, you are positive you were not checking to see if the Nightingale list was posted?

Just like you were not checking when I caught you on the steps the other day."

Betty hung her head and mumbled something unintelligible.

Jorge patted her shoulder. "That's all right. I know how you girls get about these things. You probably have not slept in a week. Am I right?"

Betty blushed. If only he knew how right. "No, I mean . . ."

"Sweet little Betty." Jorge pinched her cheek. "I should not tell you this, but I simply cannot bear to see you in this state. Betty, you are a Nightingale."

Betty's heart leaped. "I am?"

"Ab-so-lutely. You were one of my easier choices."

"Gee, thanks," Betty gushed, mentally kicking herself.

"No thanks are necessary, Senorita Berke. Just make sure you don't tell the other girls before I have a chance to post the list this afternoon."

"I won't, J—Mr. Marquez," Betty promised. Then she turned and ran out of the music building, into the golden sun. She felt like she was running on air.

Daphne opened one sleepy eye and looked at the clock. It was Saturday. Who would be pounding on her door this early in the morning? "Betty, you get it," Daphne said, rolling over. But when the knocking continued,

Daphne sat up and saw that Betty was already gone, her bed neatly made. She had a sinking feeling in her stomach as she remembered that today was the day the new Nightingales would be announced. She had a flash of the liquor from her flask spreading across the music-hall floor.

Pushing the unpleasant memory aside, she threw on a robe and yawned her way to the door.

"I woke you," Rachel said when she opened it.

"Brilliant."

"Sorry," Rachel said curtly, "but I was worried about Susan."

"Why, what's wrong with Susan?"

"She didn't come home last night."

Daphne needed a cup of coffee to really get her brain working, so it was a moment before she answered. "She left me a message that she'd be home late and not to worry."

Rachel looked relieved. "Then everything's okay. I was just worried after that bad experience she had with Randy Applewood."

Daphne yawned. "She told you about that?"

"Told me? It was Scott and I who brought her home."

Daphne's eyebrows shot up. Rachel helping Susan? Rachel *and* Scott? The last thing she wanted to wake up to was the name of her ex, Scott Hammer. She certainly didn't want to hear his name linked with Rachel's. And Susan's. Looked like her betrayers had a real coffee klatsch going.

"How come you brought her home?"
Daphne snarled.

Rachel looked at her as though the answer
was obvious. "Susan was very upset. She
needed someone with her."

"She was lucky you were around then,
wasn't she? Well, I'm sure Susan is just fine
now. Thanks for coming by." Daphne closed
the door in Rachel's face and went back to her
bedroom. Susan must have deliberately kept
Rachel and Scott's helpful presence that night
a secret. No way it could be an oversight. And
where had Susan been all night? Her message
said late, not gone forever.

As Daphne took a shower, her thoughts got
uglier and uglier. Susan was a traitor, no
doubt about it. It couldn't have happened at a
worse time, either, just when she was all uptight about the Nightingales. Please God, she
thought, don't let Susan's stupid scene with
that flask ruin my chances of making the
group.

As she got dressed she wished she could
have a drink instead of the coffee she had
been longing for earlier. Well, why not? she
reasoned. She had never had a drink this early
in the morning before, but with all that was
going on, she had a right to. It might wake her
up even better than coffee. She went to get the
bottle out of her drawer.

A little while later, Susan took a deep
breath and knocked on the door to Daphne's

suite. Telling her where she'd been all night was not going to be fun.

"Come in," Daphne's voice wafted toward her from the bedroom.

Susan steeled herself and walked in. Daphne was putting the finishing touches on her makeup. "Look who's back."

"Hi, Daphne. I just wanted to let you know I was here." Actually, Susan had been tempted to avoid Daphne, but she figured the sooner she got this confrontation over with, the sooner she could go to bed.

"Come in," Daphne said. "Where have you been?"

Realizing that the truth would only make matters worse, Susan decided to fudge a little. "It was the weirdest thing. I met Bruce while I was at the library studying for my lit course, and he told me he had taken the course last year. He said he had an old test in his room, so we went back and studied together," Susan finished in a rush.

"I see."

"And I got back late," Susan added, trying to fill the void.

"The way I heard it from your dear, dear friend Rachel, you didn't get back at all. She was so worried about you, she came pounding on my door about an hour ago to see if I knew where you were."

Susan didn't know what to say. She should have figured Rachel would be worried about her.

Then Daphne dropped her bombshell. "I guess she thought you might have been kidnapped by Randy Applewood and that she and Scott would have to rescue you again."

Susan's heart sank. This was going to be worse than she thought. "Daphne, I didn't tell you because I knew you'd react just like this. I didn't go looking for Rachel, she just happened to be there."

"And you were glad?"

"Yes, I was glad," Susan said wearily. "I was really upset."

Then Daphne unexpectedly and harshly changed tacks. "You slept with Bruce last night, didn't you?"

Perhaps Susan should not have been surprised at the bluntness of Daphne's question, but she was. "Not that it's any of your business, but no, I didn't."

"You were together all night and you just studied?" Daphne asked mockingly.

"We also played backgammon." There was no way Susan was going to share the details of Bruce's silly, sweet romantic gesture with an angry Daphne.

"Sure glad we spent all that time practicing how you were going to turn Bruce down for a date. I guess 'no' just isn't in your vocabulary."

"What a lousy thing to say." Susan's voice was trembling.

Before Daphne could go any further, though, Betty broke the tension by bounding excitedly into the room. "I just saw Jorge coming up the walk," she burbled, forcing back her excitement, "I think he's got the Nightingale list with him."

"Well, let's go see who's on it," Susan said, heading for the door without even looking to see if Daphne would follow. Susan didn't know whether she was glad or sorry that Daphne did.

When the trio arrived downstairs, they found several girls surrounding the bulletin board. Margot Williams was one of them and she was all smiles. Another girl was patting her on the back.

When Margot saw Betty coming down the hall, she called out to her, "Hey, girl, congratulations. You made it too." Betty ran over to the board as if she wanted to see her name for herself. Then she turned to Susan. "You too." Betty and Susan hugged as Daphne made her way to the bulletin board. Susan had known for a long time that Daphne wouldn't make it, but Daphne had to see for herself. Susan couldn't bear to watch her reading the list, looking over and over for the name that wasn't there.

She gave Daphne a sympathetic look. Despite their fight, she knew how much Daphne had been counting on making the Nightingales. "Daphne, I'm sure it was just because they didn't need as many altos. You'll make it next time."

"Sure you will," Betty seconded.

Rather than making her feel better, their sympathy seemed to enrage Daphne. She turned to Susan with a venomous look. "You sabotaged me. You did it on purpose."

Susan stared at her. "What are you talking about?"

"Don't try to deny it. You embarrassed me in front of Jorge on purpose."

The girls were beginning to draw an interested crowd, so Susan pulled Daphne into a corner. "Are you crazy?"

"Don't touch me," Daphne said through clenched teeth. "And don't deny it. You knocked the flask right out of my hand."

"That's what you're talking about? Get real, Daphne, I was just trying to get you to put it away."

"And I suppose that's why you said, 'Daphne, you don't deserve to be a Nightingale' You made damn sure Jorge heard it too."

"Daphne, stop it, you're scaring me. You know I never said anything like that. I would never say you didn't deserve to be a Nightingale." Susan grabbed Daphne's arms, trying to shake some sense into her. "You've been drinking again, haven't you? What's wrong with you?"

Daphne's blue eyes narrowed. "Don't play Polly Purebred with me, Susan. I am never going to forgive you for keeping me out of Nightingales." With that, she turned on her heel and ran upstairs.

Susan was shaking, but Betty was at her side in an instant. "She's pretty upset, huh?" said Betty.

"Oh Lord, yes. I knew getting into Nightingales was a big thing for her, but to accuse me of keeping her out . . . Honestly, Betty, I would never say those things she said I did."

"I know that. Just forget it," Betty advised. "She'll calm down."

"But what if she doesn't? She's been so— I don't know—out of control lately. You know how Daphne likes to get her own way. I just don't know what she'll do now that the Nightingales have turned her down on top of everything else."

"Maybe I better steer clear of the room for a while. She probably wants to be alone."

Susan looked at Betty intently. "That's nice of you." She paused for a moment. "We've given you a rough time this year, haven't we? All this talk about switching rooms."

Betty did not meet her gaze. "I admit it hasn't been the greatest rooming with Daphne. I know she would have rather stayed with you."

"Funny, I'm beginning to think leaving her was a smart move after all." Susan smiled sheepishly at Betty.

"I'm going to go over to the music building to ask Jorge when the first rehearsal is. Want to come?"

"No thanks. The only place I'm going is to bed."

Betty looked at her critically. "You do look pretty tired. Up late studying?"

"Playing for a change."

"Susan." Cathy Thomas stuck her head down the stairs. "There's a call up here for you."

Bruce! "See you later, Betty," she called as she flew up the staircase. She picked up the phone and answered in a breathless voice, "Hello?"

"Is this the backgammon queen?"

Susan laughed in delight. "Where are you? I thought you'd be halfway to Ohio by now."

"My plane was delayed, so I thought I'd make good use of my time by calling you."

"Smart boy."

"How are you feeling?"

"Tired. How about you?"

"Tired but happy. And a little scared."

"Why scared?" Susan asked.

"I'm not quite sure," Bruce said slowly. "I know you—and a lot of other people—think I'm a wild and crazy guy, but things usually don't move so fast for me."

"Are you sorry?" Susan asked, immediately defensive. "Nothing's really happened, you know, we could just forget about last night if you want to."

"Hey, hey, I'm trying to be honest and you jump all over me."

"I didn't mean to."

"We're both kind of out of it, I guess. Don't worry. Hey, they're calling my plane. I'll call you from Cleveland, okay?"

"Sure . . ." Susan could hear the buzzing of a disconnected phone line. She hung up. Bruce said don't worry and she wouldn't. She was too tired to worry. Too tired to think. She wandered back to her room, lay down on the bed, and was asleep before her head hit the pillow.

The Greek Street games couldn't really distract Daphne from her simmering fury with Susan, but they were the only distraction she could find.

These charity games were a cross between the Olympics and a children's birthday party. Each of the various fraternities and sororities had teams that participated in events like scooter races and a giant game of musical chairs. All of Greek Street had been roped off for the event and crowds were lining the barricades, cheering on their favorite participants.

Not feeling particularly sociable, Daphne just cruised past most of the events without stopping. Then she noticed Nancy Gurney and some of her Gamma friends talking animatedly on the corner. All right, Daphne thought, maybe this was her chance to fix Susan's wagon. The Gammas seemed really upset about something. Daphne drifted toward the edge of the group.

"What are we going to do?" Nancy was saying. "This isn't funny."

"It certainly isn't," said Marcia Lockett, the

Gamma secretary. "Mrs. Dunbar mentioned redoing the rec room while she was here the last time. This could blow the whole thing."

"Hey, Andrea," Daphne called, seizing her chance. Andrea was the one sister who still talked to her. "Pretty good turnout, isn't it?"

"Sure is," Andrea agreed, obviously wanting to steer her away from their private group.

"Too bad Susan couldn't make it," Daphne added blithely.

Nancy's head snapped around. "Susan? Susan Radcliffe?"

"Sure, you remember her, don't you?" Daphne smiled. "What's the matter? You all look so serious."

"Daphne," Andrea began hesitantly, "do you know Mrs. Gregory Dunbar?"

Daphne wrinkled her brow. "Dunbar? No, I don't think so. Should I?"

"She's one of our benefactors."

"That's nice." Daphne pretended to be puzzled.

"The thing is, we just got a letter from Mrs. Dunbar saying how much she wants Susan in Gamma Gamma Chi."

"Really?"

"And seeing as how you and Susan are such good friends, I thought if Susan knew Mrs. Dunbar, you might too."

"No, I don't know her," Daphne said. Then she shook her head. "Poor Susan."

"What do you mean?" Nancy interjected.

"Nothing. Look, I've got to get going."

Daphne turned to go, but as she had hoped, Andrea put a restraining hand on her shoulder. "Daphne, is there something you're not telling us?"

"Nothing I'm sure of," Daphne said slowly.

"But there is something," Marcia insisted.

Daphne nodded her head. "I don't think Susan knows this Mrs. Dunbar either," she said softly.

"But she has to know her," Nancy said. "We have the letter."

Daphne shook her head sadly. "I'm only telling you this because I know how much that letter must have upset you. But if you want my opinion, I think Susan wrote it herself."

Marcia looked shocked. "But it's on official Gamma stationery."

"I guess if she were desperate enough, she could have gotten it somewhere." Daphne shrugged.

"And was she desperate?" Andrea asked.

"I'm afraid so." Daphne lowered her voice confidentially. "She was really upset about not getting into the sorority and her parents were too. I think this must have been some way-out plan to make you reconsider."

Nancy gave her a strange look. "You're so tight with Susan, why would you tell us this?"

"Well, I didn't want to. It's just that Susan needs help so badly. I've been begging her to see a counselor or shrink, but she doesn't listen to me. Maybe if something like this came out, it would force her to get some help."

"Wow," Marcia said, "this is really heavy."

"I don't know," Nancy said. "Maybe she just did it out of spite. You know, just to get us all upset."

"Well, it is hard to figure out someone else's motives," Daphne quickly agreed.

"I don't quite know what to do about this," said Andrea. "I mean we can't just accuse her of writing this letter."

"Of course not," Daphne said, "but gettng proof should be easy enough. Just call up Mrs. Dunbar and see if she wrote it. If she didn't, you know it was Susan."

Chapter 11

"See you later," Susan said, heading for her room.

"Later," Cathy agreed. Rachel waved. They turned into the Windsor Hall lounge.

What a surprising afternoon, Susan thought to herself as she opened the door to her suite and went looking for her *Canterbury Tales*. Cathy and Rachel had really been nice to her.

She had been feeling pretty bored this morning. Sundays were never the greatest anyway, and knowing things were unsettled with Bruce didn't help. Then, of course, there was Daphne. Although she had slept away most of Saturday and Saturday night, Susan was sure that Daphne hadn't come by her room. She certainly hadn't made plans to have Sunday breakfast with Susan, the way she usually did.

By Sunday afternoon Susan was going a little stir crazy, and Rachel had noticed. When Rachel asked if she would like to go to the movie at the student union with her and Cathy

Thomas, Susan jumped at the chance. *His Girl Friday* was showing, a great old flick about two newspaper reporters, Cary Grant and Rosalind Russell. They were always playing one-upmanship, even though they had a thing for each other. Just like her and Bruce, Susan thought dreamily. At least she hoped Bruce felt that way. That phone call had been kind of a bummer. If only his plane hadn't been called at that moment. Trust the airlines to screw things up.

"Susan." Margot Williams stuck her head in the door. "There's a call for you."

"Thanks Margot," Susan said, practically flying by her. Bruce!

Instead, when she arrived huffing and puffing at the phone, the voice at the other end was Gloria's.

"Hello, dear."

Susan slipped down to the carpet, knees up, back against the wall. "Hi, Gloria. How are you? How's Daddy?"

"We're fine, but you don't sound very well."

"I don't?"

"No, and I'm sure I know the reason."

How could Gloria know about Bruce? Susan wondered "You do?"

"It's this silly spat you're having with Daphne."

Susan closed her eyes.

"Daphne called her mother and Jean called me. Susan, I don't like the reports I've been hearing."

"What did she say happened?" Would Daphne have been horrible enough to mention she had been out all night?

"She said you've been mean to her, and upsetting her. She didn't give any specifics."

Well, at least Daphne hadn't sunk that low. "Daphne and I haven't been getting along very well lately, Gloria. I made the Nightingales and she didn't. That was part of it."

"I'm sure you both have your reasons, dear, but I don't want this to continue. Jean and I love to think of you and Daphne at Hastings having fun together. You must find a way to make it up."

"All right, Gloria, I'll try," Susan said, clutching the cord.

"That's my good girl."

"Can I talk to Daddy?"

"He's on the golf course, Susan. I'll have him try you later. 'Bye, now."

"Okay, Gloria, 'bye." Susan slowly got up and replaced the receiver. She wondered fleetingly if she should have mentioned Daphne's drinking. No, Daphne really wouldn't trust her then.

Right now, however, she was going to go back to her room, find her lit book, and head over to the library. She was willing to give it one more chance with Daphne if she had to, but she wasn't willing to do it right now.

An hour later, Daphne was on her way to a better-than-nothing date with Larry Brent. Just as she closed the door to her suite, she heard the hall phone ring. Someone called Susan's name, and when Daphne reached the phone, she saw Cynthia Woyzek taking a message.

Daphne sauntered over to her.

"Hi, Cynthia," she said.

Cynthia looked up, startled.

"Was that a call for Susan?"

"Yes, do you know where she is?"

"I'm just going to meet her," Daphne said brightly. "I'll give it to her."

Cynthia shrugged, handing it over. "Be my guest."

Daphne waited until Cynthia was around the corner to open the note. *Susan—Bruce Shetland called. He can't come back till the middle of the week. Please call him.* The note gave a phone number with an Ohio area code.

I don't think she'll have time, Daphne thought, as she tore the note into tiny little pieces. She threw them into the hallway waste basket. 'Bye-'bye, Bruce.

Blue Monday, thought Susan as she sat in the Windsor Hall lounge. It was an attractive place with Oriental carpets on the floor, comfortable couches and chairs, and soothing lighting. It was especially nice to be here when it was empty, like now. Susan was rarely up early enough to see it empty, but sleeping in was just one of the things she hadn't been doing lately.

"Susan," Betty Berke interrupted her thoughts. "Are you okay?"

Susan gave her a small smile. "Sure, what's up?"

"The first Nightingale rehearsal is tonight."

"How could I forget?"

"Do you want to go over with me and Margot?"

"I'd like that. So are you excited about seeing the great Jorge in action tonight?" she teased.

"I'm sure Jorge will be interesting to work with," Betty said with great dignity.

"Just 'interesting'?" Susan asked.

"Good-bye, Susan," Betty said firmly.

Rain began to spatter against the window. Perfect, Susan sighed. The rain really fit her mood. No call from Bruce and no idea when he was coming back. She had called his dorm last night, but whoever answered said he was still gone. Bruce must really be upset with her not to call. Why, why had she said he could forget about that night if he wanted to? And did he *have* to say he was scared? She couldn't believe she had blown it this soon. Oh well, at least she had the Nightingale rehearsal to look forward to.

The Nightingales were becoming more and more important to Susan. She had had a long discussion with Bruce about her singing during the backgammon game.

"You're more enthusiastic about singing than almost anything else. Aren't you?" Bruce had said.

Trust old perceptive Bruce. When Susan looked back on her life, she could say that some of her happiest moments revolved around singing. She had missed music since coming to Hastings. Now the Nightingales were going to open that world for her again. No matter how bad she felt about Bruce, the thought of it raised her spirits.

How could Daphne possibly think I torpedoed her on purpose? Susan instinctively knew that music was just as important to Daphne as it was to her. She hoped it was just the liquor talking, and hoped it wouldn't be talking too much longer. Susan swung her long legs off the couch. It was time to go find Daphne and straighten all this out.

She headed up to Daphne's room. Daphne was just locking her door.

"Daphne, can I talk to you for a second?"

Daphne shrugged and reopened the door. "Sure, let's go inside."

Susan took off her glasses and faced her squarely. "I talked to Gloria last night. She told me that you were upset, and I know how you felt about not getting into Nightingales, but you don't really think I knocked that bottle out of your hand on purpose, do you?"

Daphne's face was impassive. "I think I have plenty of things to be angry about, Susan," she said calmly. "I spend hours and hours helping you plan how to turn down Bruce—"

"Oh, it wasn't hours and hours, Daphne."

"It was wasted time if you were just going to fall into his arms the minute you saw him."

"Okay, I'm sorry, I wouldn't have wasted

your time if I knew I was going to give in, but—"

"And then there was the whole thing with Rachel and Scott," Daphne interrupted. "How could you stand to be around them after what they did to me?"

"They didn't really do anything to you, they just fell for each other."

"But you're supposed to be my friend. If you had an enemy, I would be on your side, not theirs."

"I know you would."

"So, I think you could do the same for me."

"I guess . . . I—" Susan stuttered, but Daphne didn't wait for her to finish.

Smiling broadly, she said, "I knew you'd see it my way, old buddy. See, if we try we can work things out."

How did she do it, Susan wondered? Daphne could turn her arguments inside out and suddenly be smiling because she was back in charge.

"Now that we have all that worked out, I've got a favor to ask you, Susan."

"A favor?"

"You know how the Phi Delts have a Wild Wednesday party on the first Wednesday of the month?"

Susan nodded. Wednesday was a big date night on campus because once Wednesday was over the weekend was in sight. The Phi Delt fraternity used this as an excuse to have an open party once a month and they were reputed to be super.

"Well, Larry Brent asked me to go to the party, but he wanted me to get a date for a friend of his. Naturally, I thought of you."

Susan shook her head. "I don't want to, Daphne. Bruce will probably be back by then. I want to leave myself open."

"Have you heard from him?" Daphne asked.

"No," admitted Susan, "but I may have missed his call."

"I'm sure someone would have left you a message."

"Well maybe he'll just see me when he gets back."

"Maybe," Daphne said doubtfully. "I personally think it would be a good idea if you went out with Larry's friend. I mean, it would show Bruce you weren't waiting around for him, and it would probably be a lot of fun."

"I don't think so, Daphne, but thanks anyway."

"Sure, well, think about it. You can let me know anytime."

"I'll think about it. Don't count on me though."

Susan, Betty, and Margot were all in high spirits when they arrived at the music building. They were anxious to start their careers as Nightingales.

"Betty, do you know how soon we'll be expected to learn some of the Nightingales' standard songs?" Margot asked as they hung up their coats.

"No, but Jorge will be telling us all that." Betty turned pink. She scanned the auditorium looking for Jorge.

"Over there," Susan laughed, "talking to the accompanist."

"Who?" Betty asked, not fooling anyone. "Oh. Jorge. I think maybe I'll go see if he needs help with anything."

Susan felt someone staring at her, and when she turned around, she saw Nancy Gurney and Andrea Matson looking her way and whispering. They didn't seem very friendly.

Now don't get paranoid, Susan told herself. But it was hard not to. She had already had to give up her dream of being a Gamma. Nancy was the president of the Nightingales and could make things rough for her here too, if she wanted. To avoid them, Susan decided to join Margot. Even in the midst of their conversation, she could still feel Nancy's eyes boring into the back of her head.

"So what do you think?" Nancy was asking Andrea.

"She doesn't look very guilty," Andrea observed. "Of course, she may just be good at covering up. A real criminal would be."

"When are we going to hear from Mrs. Dunbar?" asked Nancy.

"Didn't you hear? She didn't answer our calls because she's away on a cruise. We finally got hold of her housekeeper."

"Great," Nancy groaned. "Now what?"

"Well, it's not too bad. She'll be back in a

day or two, so we can see whether or not she wrote the letter then."

"But in the meantime, how are we supposed to act toward Susan? I'm the president of Nightingales. I should be welcoming her to her first rehearsal."

Andrea considered this. "It is innocent until proven guilty in this country."

"I guess," Nancy replied. "But let's wait until we talk to Mrs. Dunbar. Susan may not be around long enough for a hello. Just a good-bye."

Chapter 12

Now I'm starting to get mad, Susan thought. Here it is Tuesday night and I still haven't heard from Bruce. Susan was pulling on her sweat pants and a sweatshirt. Cathy Thomas had suggested several times that Susan go running with her and today Susan had so much nervous tension she decided to give it a shot.

Anger wasn't the only emotion Susan wanted to get out of her system. She was also hurt that Bruce could drop her so casually, and surprised to discover how much she cared. Darn it all, she thought, I won't go falling in love with him. I won't!

She tried to muster her fury. *That's* the emotion she needed right now. Bruce Shetland, big talker, she thought as she slipped her blond hair into a ponytail. Moonlight and roses, but the minute it looked like it might turn serious, he takes a powder. Susan fiercely knotted her running shoes. Well, if he thinks I'm just going to sit around here waiting for him, he's crazy!

With that, Susan slammed the door to her

suite and marched over to Daphne's room.

"Hi." Daphne looked up lazily from her studying. "What are you decked out for?"

"I'm going running," Susan said curtly.

"Running?" Daphne snickered. "Since when are you a runner?"

Susan ignored her. "What's the name of Larry Brent's friend? The guy you want to fix me up with for the Phi Delt party?"

"Ed Ellerbee."

"I don't know him." Susan frowned. "What's he like?"

"I haven't met him either. He's a junior and supposedly decent looking."

"All right, I'll go."

"You will?" Daphne said triumphantly. She jumped up from the couch and gave her friend a little hug. "What made you change your mind?"

Susan untangled herself from Daphne's embrace. "Because I decided it's stupid to sit around here waiting for Bruce to call."

"That's right," Daphne agreed emphatically. "Now how about you forget this stupid running idea and we go over to the student union for a break."

"No thanks, I want to run."

"Susan," Daphne said with exaggerated patience, "you barely like to walk. You made Gloria's chauffeur come and pick us up from school whenever Gloria wasn't using him, and Briarwood was only a mile away from where we lived."

"That's the trouble with you, Daphne. You

still remember all the things I did when I was a twerpy eight-year-old. Now I'm eighteen and I'd like to try running." She turned to leave.

"Wait a minute, I wanted to ask you about the Nightingale practice. How did it go?"

Susan turned back. "It was fine, except for one thing. Nancy Gurney and a couple of the other Gammas really gave me the cold shoulder."

"The cold shoulder?" Daphne inquired, looking perplexed. "But why should they do that?"

"I don't know."

"Did they say anything?" Daphne persisted.

"No, that was the funny part. They didn't say a thing, although I'd swear Andrea Matson looked like she was dying to ask me a question."

"I wouldn't feel too bad. They were probably too busy to be polite, first rehearsal and all."

"I don't think that was it. Even Margot noticed that Nancy was introducing the new members around, but she wouldn't even look at me."

Daphne shrugged. "You are a Gamma reject, they probably aren't crazy about you."

"They don't have to like me, but they don't have to be rude." Susan glanced at her watch. "Cathy is waiting for me. I gotta go. Just tell Ed to give me a call."

"I will. You're making a smart move," Daphne called as Susan left the suite.

* * *

As soon as Susan was safely downstairs, Daphne hurried to the hall telephone. She flipped through the campus directory and found the Gamma Gamma Chi house number. When a pledge answered the ring, she asked for Andrea.

"Andrea, this is Daphne Riesling."

"Daphne," Andrea said in a surprised tone, "what can I do for you?"

"I was just talking to Susan Radcliffe's parents, and they asked me to find out if you had any further word on who wrote that letter."

"I'm afraid so, Daphne. I just talked to Mrs. Dunbar an hour ago and she says she never wrote us at all. She's been away on a cruise."

"That's what I was afraid of. Listen, Andrea, I know you must be furious with Susan, but her parents hoped that you wouldn't say anything to her. They've been talking to a shrink they're going to send her to in Boston and he thinks any confrontations would be devastating."

"I don't know, some of the girls are really angry about this."

"I can believe it, but she's sick, Andrea. I think they can all understand that."

"Look, Daphne, we're having a meeting tonight and I'll explain the situation. I'm sure the girls will respect the Radcliffes' feelings."

"Good, they'll be very grateful. Thanks a lot, Andrea."

That was close, Daphne thought as she hung up the phone. She jumped a little as the phone shrilled again.

"Windsor Hall, second floor."

"Susan Radcliffe, please."

Bruce, no doubt about it. She wondered briefly if she could disguise her voice, but she wasn't sure she could pull it off. "Bruce," she said sweetly. "it's Daphne. Susan isn't here."

"Where is she?" he asked curtly.

"I don't think I'm at liberty to say," she replied mysteriously.

"Why not?"

"Susan wouldn't like it if I told *you.*"

"Sure, Daphne," Bruce said in a disgusted tone of voice. "Then just tell her I'm going to be back early tomorrow night and I'll see her then."

"I hate to be the one to tell you this, Bruce, but Susan already has a date for tomorrow."

Bruce exploded. "With who?"

"Ed Ellerbee."

"Who the hell is Ed Ellerbee?"

"She's going to the Phi Delt Wild Wednesday party with him."

"That's great. I leave for a few days and . . . oh, never mind. Just tell Susan I called—if you think you can handle the responsibility."

Daphne jerked the receiver away as it slammed in her ear. Of all the nerve. She slammed down the phone and stalked to her room Just one more humiliation to chalk up to Susan and her nasty new friends. Daphne wasn't sorry at all about what she'd done. Not one bit.

"Then what did he say?" Susan was in Daphne's room getting ready for their double date. She'd been upset ever since Daphne had told her she'd missed a call from Bruce.

"I told you what he said a hundred times, at least. He asked where you were, I said you were out. He said he'd see you tomorrow, I told him you had a date. If I shouldn't have done that, I'm sorry."

"No, I've decided it's all right," Susan said, putting Daphne's green linen jacket over her shirt and jeans. "He never got in touch with me, so why should I sit around waiting for him?"

Daphne sighed. "Right, right, a million times right." She went over to the closet mirror and began applying her eye makeup.

"He didn't say anything about trying to reach me before, did he?"

Daphne put down her mascara and picked up her lipstick. "No, he did not."

"So why should I worry about him?"

"Enough!" Daphne yelled. "Forget about him. You have a date tonight and you are doubling with me. If you keep going on like this, you're going to ruin four people's evenings. What are you going to do, ask Ed if you should have gone out with Bruce tonight?"

"No, of course not. Be quiet." Susan looked

at herself in the mirror. Green was definitely
one of her best colors. "You're right, I'll
forget about him. At least for this evening."

"How about forever? The guy's a creep."

Susan thought back to Bruce's sweet kisses,
his crazy, funny conversations. He certainly
wasn't a creep, but he was inconsiderate and
the next time she saw him she was going to
tell him so.

Chapter 13

Even Susan had to admit Bruce was acting like a creep when she saw him, less than an hour later.

Her evening had started out well enough. Ed Ellerbee was a tall, quiet guy with a receding hairline. Nothing to get excited about, but not instant death either. Susan, Ed, Larry, and Daphne had driven over to the Phi Delt house, where the beer was flowing like water and the laughs were coming a mile a minute.

A rock band was playing loudly in the corner when they arrived, but the place was so jammed, the only people who could really hear were those dancing around the bandstand. Susan and Ed were shouting at each other about the latest Springsteen album, when Susan looked up and saw Bruce coming through the doorway.

Delight, anger, and surprise coursing through her, Susan looked directly in Bruce's eyes. Instead of coming over, however, Bruce just nodded curtly and walked right past her.

All Susan could do was stare as he went over to Daphne and Larry and sat down next to them. Susan headed straight for the three of them as Ed trailed, unsuspecting, behind her.

"So, Daphne, how goes it?" Bruce inquired.

Daphne looked more and more bewildered as Bruce ignored Susan.

"Daphne, you're not answering me, honey, how are you?"

"Fine."

"Aren't you going to introduce me to your friend here?"

"This is Larry Brent."

Larry looked at Bruce oddly, shook his hand, and resumed his conversation. A moment later, though, Bruce was butting in again.

"So, were you busy while I was away?"

Daphne glared at him. "Bruce, you're being rude. I'm trying to talk to my date."

"But I want to know what you've been up to since I left," Bruce persisted.

Susan was so mystified by Bruce's behavior that she almost didn't hear poor Ed asking her if she wanted another drink.

Waving him distractedly away, she said, "Sure, that would be great." What in the world was Shetland trying to do?

"You know what I think you've been doing?" Bruce pestered.

"Hey, pal," Larry interrupted, completely fed up, "why don't you take a hike?"

"Not yet, 'pal.' " All this time, Bruce had been staring exclusively at Daphne. "I think you've been doing some nasty things," he told her. His gaze didn't falter.

"I don't know what you're talking about," Daphne protested, visibly upset.

Susan wasn't sure what this was all about either, but she was sure she'd had enough of it. Insinuating herself between Bruce and Daphne, so that he had to acknowledge her, she put on her best ice-princess act. "Bruce," she said, "I think you owe Daphne an apology."

Finally, Bruce stood up and gave Susan his attention. "In your dreams, Susan. I have the feeling Daphne has been jerking us both around real good."

"I don't know what you're talking about, Bruce, but this obviously isn't the place for your wild accusations."

"You're standing up for her?"

"Why shouldn't I?"

Bruce grabbed Susan's hand. "That's it, you're coming with me."

"Get your hands off her, you eccentric little creep," Daphne shot back.

Bruce clutched his heart and staggered. " 'Eccentric little creep'? *Moi?* Oh Daphne, you have cut me to the quick." He stifled a cry of pain with the back of his hand.

"Bravo," yelled one of the frat brothers, inspiring a few others to whistle appreciatively.

Bruce bowed modestly. "Please, please, it was nothing," he murmured.

Susan's head was spinning. "Bruce Shetland, what is going on here?"

Bruce turned to her. "I called you Sunday night. Even left a message with Cynthia Woyzek, but"—he spread his hands—"no return call from Susan. So, I asked myself, has Susan developed a phone allergy? Or is this Woyzek character the sort of social deviant who takes messages just so she can tear them up? Then the next time I call, your 'friend' Daphne very conveniently tells me you're going to be out with someone else tonight. Okay, I say. I can take a hint. Maybe I'm not irresistible—but just in case something fishy's going on, I have a face-to-face chat with Cynthia when I get back into town. Surprise, surprise. Cynthia tells me she gave my message to Daphne, who conveniently volunteered to pass it on."

Susan turned her huge blue-eyed gaze on Daphne. "You did that?"

"I can't believe you'd take his word over mine!" Daphne exclaimed shrilly.

"Let's go," Bruce said to Susan.

Susan bit her lip in confusion. "But I came with Ed." A moment later, she found a solution. She turned to Daphne. "No wonder you were in such a hurry to fix me up. Well, this is your lucky night, Daphne. Now you've got two dates."

Before anything else could happen, Bruce slipped his arm around Susan's shoulder and propelled her out of the crowd.

Once they got outside, Bruce took off his cotton sweater and gave it to Susan. "Here, put this on."

Susan slipped off her jacket, pulled on Bruce's sweater and her jacket over that. She was still freezing.

"I think there's only one way to warm you up." Bruce put his arms around her and gave her a gentle kiss. "Better?"

She nodded. "Much. But maybe you should tell me what's going on here. I'm all confused."

"I know the feeling."

"Tell me everything. From the beginning."

"I guess the beginning would be the airport."

"You hung up on me," Susan accused.

"Not true. Logan Airport is a toll call and my time ran out. Since they were calling my plane, I figured I'd just talk to you from home."

Susan met his eyes unflinchingly. "You said you were feeling scared."

"I was. I was also being honest. Something you may not be familiar with in your relationships," he replied.

"I guess you're right about that," Susan sighed.

"So then I got to Gates Mills. My mother has been in pretty bad shape since the divorce. She doesn't go out much. Just sort of sits around and feels bad."

"That's terrible." Susan squeezed his arm.

"Once I got there she was like a drowning woman clinging to a life preserver. She didn't want me to leave."

"What did you do?"

"I finally convinced her to go back to her therapist. She used to go regularly, even before the divorce. But she said she didn't like telling him depressing things. My mother"—Bruce shook his head affectionately—"she's one of a kind. Anyway, she had her first session while I was there, and I think it'll make a big difference."

"You're a good son." Susan smiled at him.

"Thanks, that's just the reputation I want spread around Hastings: Bruce Shetland—Good Son. Favorite of dogs and little old ladies."

"And some not-so-old ladies," Susan said, pulling his head down and giving him a kiss.

"My, aren't we bold tonight? I've created a monster."

"You don't like forward girls?"

"You, I like backwards, forwards, sideways—" He was stopped by Susan's lips.

"I'm hungry," Susan said, interrupting their kiss.

"What is this? Kissing me reminds you of chopped liver?"

"No." Susan giggled. "But I haven't gotten a decent meal out of you yet. Why don't we talk over some food?"

Bruce helped her off the bench. "Okay, let's take the car and see where we wind up."

Once they were out on the road, Bruce

brought up the subject of Daphne. "I knew you were too polite to just walk out on a date, so I decided I'd better get to you through Daphne."

"I know you'll find this hard to believe," Susan began earnestly, "but there really is more to Daphne than, well, the girl who rerouted your phone messages. She's been under a lot of pressure lately."

Bruce shook his head. "Everybody's got pressures, Susan. You just can't make excuses for people who pull things like Daphne pulled."

"All right, I admit I never really believed Daphne could be so mean and nasty—at least not to me. But, gee, Bruce, Daphne and I have been friends a long time. We've got a real history together. I can't abandon her now."

"Susan, just because you're making a few new friends like—Rachel, was it?—and me is no reason for Daphne to act like you've abandoned her. I'm sorry, but her reaction is all out of proportion."

Susan picked at her fingernail and watched the handsome residences of Hastings Valley roll by her window. "That's not exactly what I meant," she said unsurely. "I'm worried about her . . . About her drinking."

Bruce whistled softly. "She drinks too? And you were ready to move back in with this girl?"

"She always drank some in high school, and she never seemed to have any trouble with it, but now . . . Bruce, she was drunk when she went to that Nightingale audition. So drunk she dropped her flask in front of Jorge Marquez. So drunk that she blames me for it, and thinks she heard me say she didn't deserve to be a Nightingale. I wouldn't even think something like that."

"Maybe that's what Daphne thinks herself," Bruce said thoughtfully.

"Maybe. I don't know. All I know is I'm worried about her and nothing I say these days is ever right when it comes to Daphne." Susan felt tears welling behind her eyes. "I keep thinking maybe if I try a little harder. If only I could get her to talk about it. But most of the time when I'm around her now, I just feel suffocated." She pressed her face against the seat cushion. "Sometimes I'm so ashamed," she whispered.

"Shh-shh." Bruce patted her shoulder. "One thing you have to realize about alcoholics—"

"I didn't say she was an alcoholic."

"Susan."

"All right. I guess she probably is."

Bruce was silent for a moment. Then he went on. "One thing about alcoholics. As much as you want to help, you can't make yourself responsible for their drinking. You can support them. You can be their friend. But, ultimately, they have to help themselves. If you try to take all Daphne's problems on your own shoulders, you'll just go crazy. And you might not end up helping her, either."

Susan looked at him. "You sound like you know what you're talking about."

He nodded. "I lost a good friend to drinking and driving. It took two years in Alanon for me to shut up all those 'what if's.' "

"I'm sorry." Susan clasped her hands in her lap. "Bruce, do you think Daphne and I will ever be friends again, like we were?"

Bruce shrugged helplessly. "I don't know if there's hope for you and Daphne. But I do know there's hope for you and me."

"That's a given."

"Thank you," said Bruce, running his hand over her sleek blond hair.

Susan flicked on the radio and twisted the dial until she found a rock station that she liked. "You know what scares me the most about all this?"

"What's that?"

"I was just like her. I was a Daphne clone."

Bruce pulled the car over to the curb. He cupped Susan's face in his hands. "Now listen and listen good. I admit for a long time you did a pretty good imitation of a Daphne clone. You could be as mean and vacant and bitchy as Daphne on her best day. That was all a masquerade, though. It was a costume you were wearing because you were afraid to wear your real Susan clothes. But you better not think for one minute I'm going to let you change back. Not when I was lucky enough to find out what you're really like."

Susan looked at him with tears in her eyes. "How come you know so much?"

"I just do," he said, taking her in his arms and kissing her passionately.

Chapter 14

Most of the breakfast crowd had cleared out of the cafeteria, but Susan, Rachel, Cathy, and Agatha Mitchell were sitting around having second cups of coffee and rehashing last night's events. Cathy's boyfriend, John Wickland, and Agatha's, Lance Tuchman, were Phi Delts. Naturally, both girls had witnessed the whole scene. Rachel was dying because she hadn't been there and Susan wanted to know what had happened after she left.

"Honey," Agatha said in her thick Texas drawl, "Daphne is going to be scared to show her face in public after that shindig."

"Yep," agreed Cathy. "I think she had too much drink even before the thing with Bruce. She was really chugging it down!"

Aggie leaned forward, eager to dish. "As soon as you left she started bad-mouthing you, just kind of squawkin' and finally someone said, 'Hey, she sounds like Daffy Duck.' Everybody started laughin' and Daphne took off like a bat outa hell."

"Gosh, she must have been so humiliated," Susan said.

Rachel stirred some more sugar into her coffee. "I have to give you credit for being so sympathetic. She sure didn't turn out to be much of a friend."

Susan's face flamed and she quickly lowered her head. She thought about all the times she'd been so mean to Rachel. "What happened to Larry?" Rachel asked.

"Never mind Larry," Susan broke in. "What happened to poor Ed?" That question had been bothering her all morning.

"Poor Ed and poor Larry went back to the bar and got themselves stinkin' drunk," Agatha recounted. "They stumbled around for a while until someone took pity on 'em and drove 'em home."

"I hope I didn't embarrass Ed too badly by leaving early," Susan said, "but there was nothing I could do about it."

"You sure couldn't, gal," Agatha agreed. "Lance and I were watchin'. That Bruce Shetland would have picked you up and thrown you over his shoulder if you hadn't gone with him."

"Bruce definitely does things his own way." Susan nodded.

"He's a neat guy," Rachel said. "See that you treat him right."

"You doubt that I would?" Susan smiled.

Rachel turned serious for a moment. "Not that long ago I would have felt sorry for any guy that liked you, Susan. But you've changed, you really have."

Cathy took a final sip of juice. "I'm with

Rachel. What was it," she teased, "the power of love?"

"Partly. Maybe I just opened my eyes," Susan said shyly. "I'm almost as surprised as you are. If anyone had told me a month ago I'd be sitting in the cafeteria with the three of you, I'd have laughed in his face."

"Or spit in it," Agatha said slyly. "That was more your style."

Susan smiled. "You can't get a rise out of me. This is the new, improved Susan, and as Bruce once said, 'accept no substitutes.' "

"I don't know about you guys, but I've got to get to class," said Cathy. The other girls agreed and started gathering their belongings.

"Go ahead," Susan told them. "I don't have a class for an hour." After the others had clattered out, Susan made her way over to Cynthia Woyzek, who was wiping off the tables. She tapped her on the shoulder.

"Susan," Cynthia said, startled.

"Can I talk to you for a second?"

"I guess." Cynthia shrugged. "What's up?"

"I just wanted to thank you for telling Bruce about that message you took for me. The one Daphne asked for. It cleared up a lot of trouble between us."

"No big deal."

"It was to me, Cynthia, and I . . . I'm sorry if I've been obnoxious to you all year." Susan hadn't known how hard it would be to say these words. Cynthia's stony expression didn't help much either.

"I guess I should accept your apology and your thanks, only I didn't tell Bruce about the message for your sake. I told him because I think he's a good guy. To tell you the truth, I haven't the faintest idea what he sees in you. Since I did you a favor, though, would you do one for me?"

"Sure, what?" Susan said, almost inaudibly.

"When you come through the line in the morning and I have about fifty million Hastingsites to feed, don't ask for cold milk to go on your cereal. Because every time you do that, I really and truly feel like tossing the whole tray of oatmeal in your face. Trouble is, one of these mornings I might just do it. You know what I mean?" What that, Cynthia turned her back on Susan and began mopping another table.

Susan watched her for a minute. Then she turned and hurried out of the cafeteria, tears in her eyes. I deserved that, she thought. I've hurt a lot of people in my time and now I know how it feels to get hurt back.

"I haven't seen Daphne all day." Susan complained. "I think she's avoiding me."

"I wouldn't be surprised," Bruce agreed. The Nightingales were having their regular Thursday night rehearsal and Bruce was walking Susan over to the music building.

"She's going to have to see me eventually and it had better be soon. We've got a lot to talk about," she said.

"You know I'm not president of Daphne's fan club, but I almost feel sorry for her."

"What?" Susan looked at him with surprise.

"People were really talking about her today, about how she streaked out of the Phi Delt house. She's not very popular, you know."

"And since I was her shadow, I guess I'm not either."

Bruce gave her that crooked grin. "Ah, but that's all going to change now. You're the girl-friend of Bruce Shetland. People are bound to treat you with more respect."

"Oh, I'm your girlfriend now, am I? I don't remember anyone consulting me on that," Susan teased.

"You kissed me, young lady. You kissed me lots of times last night. In fact, you even initi-ated several of those kisses. That makes you my girlfriend; ask anybody."

Susan started to laugh. "Besides, they all saw you burst into the Phi Delt house, ready to save me from the clutches of Ed Ellerbee."

Bruce grinned back. "I feel sort of bad about old Ed. An innocent bystander. Anyway, I just couldn't help racing over to the Phi Delt house after Cynthia told me she had passed my message to Daphne."

At the mention of Cynthia's name, Susan sobered. Really, it was too humiliating to think about, much less to share with Bruce. Before she could stop herself, though, the words came tumbling out.

"I thanked Cynthia this morning, and then I apologized to her for being so crummy to her all year. You know, treating her like she was an indentured servant or something, just because she was a scholarship student and worked in the cafeteria."

"What did she say?"

Susan hung her head. She couldn't meet Bruce's gaze. "Basically, she said I was too rude and obnoxious to forgive. Only she said it a little more creatively than that. Make that a lot more."

Bruce put his arm around her shoulders. "That must have been hard to hear. But don't worry, you're starting over now and you have the perfect role model for being good, kind, and sweet: me."

" 'Good, kind and sweet,' huh? Why don't you try manipulative and boorish?" Susan's voice was level, but she could feel that old familiar anger waiting in the wings.

"Manipulative and boorish. I think I like the sound of that." Bruce gave her a squeeze. "You know why I'm crazy about you?"

"No," Susan answered, grumpily.

"Because you're so hard to push around. Everyone else just melts like butter when they're around me. You melt like a porcupine."

"Porcupines don't melt."

"Exactly!" Bruce beamed. Then his face got serious. "Susan."

"Yes."

"I didn't really mean all that stuff about

upper-class mentality and role models. I mean, I think you're fine just the way you are."

"High praise," Susan snorted, "but it's a good thing you didn't mean it, because from now on Susan isn't modeling herself on anyone but Susan."

"Hear, hear," Bruce approved. "Pip, pip and jolly good."

Susan let her anger go with a little laugh.

The two walked silently around the lake then, hand in hand, until they reached the music building.

"Have a nice sing," Bruce said, kissing her lightly on the forehead.

"I will."

"Should I pick you up afterward?"

"Sure, if you want to."

"I want to. I'll just go to the library and study until you're done. Then we can go to Mayberry's or something and grab a bite to eat."

Susan just shook her head. "I'll believe that when I see it. We never got around to the food last night, either."

"My kisses are far more nourishing than food."

"I hope so, because if it was up to you, that's all the nourishment I would get."

"I'm determined to show the world you can live on love," Bruce said giving her another kiss. Susan watched him skip down the steps of the music building.

Love! He said "love." Not that you could

take Bruce seriously, but still, you never knew. Susan herself had the sneaking suspicion that what she was feeling could easily be love.

As soon as she entered the music building, Susan saw Betty Berke waving in her direction and motioning her to come sit down.

"Hi Betty, how's it going?"

"Okay, I heard about last night," said Betty.

"Have you seen Daphne?" Susan asked. "I've been looking for her all day."

"She got up real early and said she was going downtown."

"That figures. She's probably hit every store in Boston by now. When the going gets tough, the tough go shopping. That's practically Daphne's motto."

Their conversation was interrupted by the appearance of Jorge Marquez on the stage. "As we discussed last time, ladies, the reason for spring tryouts is so that you new members can have a chance to work with the singers you'll be replacing next year. The Nightingales have been asked to sing "Greensleeves" at graduation, so that is the song we'll be working on. Now, let me read off the pairings so each of you newcomers will know who you're going to be working with."

Susan's heart sank when she heard her name being called. "Susan Radcliffe and Nancy Gurney," Jorge said.

"Swell," Susan muttered. If Nancy kept giving her the silent treatment, she'd never learn a note of anything.

"All right," Jorge continued. "Everyone on stage now. Sopranos to my right. Altos to my left. Newcomers, stand next to your partners. Come on, *vamos.*"

Susan reluctantly left her seat and walked over to Nancy. Nancy shoved the music in her hand without so much as a word.

"Thank you," Susan said sweetly, but Nancy averted her head.

For the next two hours, Jorge led them patiently through the harmonies for "Greensleeves." Since almost everyone was familiar with the song, rehearsal went smoothly. Susan was impressed with the way Jorge handled the group, firmly, but with humor.

"I think we can break now," Jorge said after they'd finally sung the song all the way through without stopping.

Susan had one question about the time signature that she wanted to ask Nancy, but her stormy expression gave her pause. For a moment, Susan was tempted to forget the whole thing, but then she decided she had better deal with the situation now, before it got any stranger.

Before Nancy could join the other girls clearing the stage, Susan pulled her off to one corner. "Nancy," she asked, "is something wrong? You seem really angry with me?"

"I'm not supposed to talk about it," Nancy snapped. "I'd hate to injure your poor little psyche."

"What are you talking about?"

"Don't pretend you don't know. It was a

lousy stunt and I don't care what anybody says, I think you knew exactly what you were doing."

Susan shook her head. "You have totally lost me."

"Really? Does the name Mrs. Gregory Dunbar ring a bell?"

How could Nancy know about the letter? Thoughts were racing through Susan's mind. Daphne agreed not to mail it. Then Susan paled. But maybe she'd lied.

"That's a guilty look on your face if I ever saw one," Nancy crowed triumphantly.

Several girls had gathered to watch the fireworks. Now Andrea and Betty joined the circle.

"Nancy." Andrea touched her friend's shoulder. "We weren't supposed to say anything. We promised Daphne."

"Daphne?" Susan looked at Andrea. "What did she tell you?"

Andrea tried to play peacemaker. "She just said that you wrote that letter from Mrs. Dunbar because you were so unhappy about not making the sorority and that your parents were going to make you see a shrink about it."

"I don't believe this," Susan said, raking her fingers through her straight blond hair. "And what excuse did Daphne give for her name being in it?"

Andrea looked puzzled. "What are you talking about? Her name wasn't even mentioned. The letter was all about you."

Susan took a deep breath and tried to calm

herself. "Listen, you've got to believe me. I had nothing to do with that letter. It was Daphne's idea and I told her I thought it was a lousy one. Supposedly, the letter was going to be about both of us, but obviously Daphne took her name off of it and left mine on."

"You expect us to believe that?" Nancy sneered.

"It's the truth," Susan swore, near tears.

"Is there some way you can prove it?" Andrea asked more gently.

Susan racked her brain. "Not really."

"I think I can prove it." Betty stepped forward.

"You know about this too?" Andrea asked.

"I didn't think much of it at the time," Betty said, twisting a tissue she was carrying, "but a couple of weeks ago I saw a letter on Gamma stationery sitting on Daphne's desk."

"You *saw* it?" Nancy asked, eyebrows raised.

"I read it," Betty admitted softly. "It was about Susan, but it was typed on Daphne's typewriter. Then the next time I came back to the room, it was gone."

"There, you see," Susan said, "that's proof." Then she had a flash. "And you can ask a guy on your staff named John Reed about it. He was there when Daphne came into the Gamma house to steal the stationery."

Andrea finally looked convinced. "I guess we do owe you an apology," she said. "We're sorry, aren't we, Nancy?"

Nancy grudgingly added her own apology.

"Well, since rehearsal's over, I'm leaving," Susan said. "I'm going to find Daphne and settle this once and for all." Then she hurried out.

"Gee, I'm glad that's over," Betty said to no one in particular.

"I wouldn't exactly say that," Nancy contradicted, looking at her in a very unfriendly manner.

"What do you mean?"

"You're a little sneak, you know that?" Nancy was a tall husky girl and loomed over Betty.

"I didn't do anything."

"That's right," Nancy said, "you didn't do anything. Daphne was going to make the Gammas look like fools. You knew about it and you never said a word."

"That wasn't very nice," Andrea interjected. "As president of the Nightingales, I think I should inform you that all new members are on probation. Usually everyone makes it, but this time I have a feeling someone won't." Looking straight at Betty, Nancy turned on her heel and walked away. Andrea followed right behind her.

Tears blurred Betty's eyes as she stumbled backstage. There, amid broken props, tools, and other assorted debris, Betty sat down on a wooden box and began to cry. This was terrible. The one thing she had been looking forward to at Hastings after her breakup with Mitch was singing in the Nightingales. Now she was going to be kicked out, or at the very least made miserable.

"Betty, *pobrecita*, why are you crying?"

Betty looked up and saw Jorge's sweet, sympathetic smile. That made her cry all the harder.

Stepping over a battered old stool and a few cartons, he joined Betty on the wooden crate. "*Che, flaca*, tell Jorge what's wrong."

Jorge patted Betty's thin little shoulder as the words came spilling out. Betty felt she wasn't making much sense, but Jorge seemed to understand.

"Nancy spoke out of anger," he said kindly. "You have a wonderful voice; we would hardly ask you to leave."

Betty looked up. Her eyes felt puffy and she was sure her nose was as red as her hair. "You wouldn't?"

"Of course not."

As he smiled down at her, Betty thought he had the kindest, most wonderful face she had ever seen.

Chapter 15

Susan darted out of the music building and set off at a run through the well-lit campus. Going out running with Cathy the last couple days had given her a little more stamina, and when she finally couldn't run anymore, she still walked at a fast clip.

As she ran, her head swam with images of Daphne writing the letter to the Gammas with just her name on it. "Accidentally" telling Gloria that Bruce had no social connections. Taking Bruce's message from Cynthia and throwing it away. Running her finger around a wine-glass. Then came images from an earlier era. Two little blond girls with matching pigtails, who looked alike enough to pass for sisters. Playing together, giggling about boys. Sharing high-school pranks.

But something bothered Susan about these pictures. Everything Susan remembered so clearly featured only the two of them. No friends, no siblings, not even parents. Susan and Daphne. Daphne and Susan. People linking their names like they weren't even two separate people.

Exhausted, Susan threw herself on the grass outside Windsor Hall. She breathed in the fragrance of the warm spring night. She heard the crickets singing and the pounding of her heart.

When had it all changed? When had she and Susan gone from friends to ruler and subject? Susan stood up and brushed the grass off of her jeans. It had been a long while coming, but it was time to confront Daphne.

Susan marched into Windsor Hall and bounded up the stairs. She slowed a little as she approached Daphne's suite. The door was ajar, so instead of knocking she walked right in.

From the common room she could see Daphne in her bedroom hanging up clothes. Summer things, shorts and tank tops, lay scattered on the floor, their price tags still attached. Susan knew Daphne all too well.

"Looks like you did a little shopping today," she said as she stepped over a blouse and entered the bedroom.

For a second, pure panic twisted Daphne's features, but then she composed herself. She treated Susan to a plastic smile. "I thought I deserved it after the lousy night I had."

"I think you deserve more than that."

Daphne continued to put clothes on satin hangers and place them in the big mirrored closet. "I suppose you're all hot and bothered because I forgot to give you that message from Bruce."

"Forgot, Daphne?"

Daphne whirled around to face her. "What

do you want me to say, I didn't forget? All right, I didn't, but you don't seem to understand that I did this for you, Susan. Bruce Shetland is just some weird guy who's going to dump you the minute someone a little more unusual comes along."

"So you wanted to break us up for my own good?"

"Yes."

"And what was your reason for sending that letter about me to the Gamma house. Was that for my own good, too?"

Daphne froze, statue-like, with a shocked look on her face. Susan almost felt sorry for her, but she told herself this was no time to be soft.

"Daphne, you're not saying anything," she prodded. "You always used to think on your feet. You must be slipping."

"I was mad at you," she finally muttered.

"I can't hear you, Daphne."

"I said I was mad," Daphne yelled. "You were getting tight with Rachel Pirnie and I wasn't going to let you get away with it. You seem to have forgotten who your real friends are."

" 'Real friends.' Real friends? Don't you mean my *one* real friend, Daphne Riesling?" Susan emphasized the singular.

"I've been a better friend to you than creeps like Pirnie and Thomas," she said, digging her fists into her hips.

"Oh, Daphne. With things the way they are between us, I'd hardly call us friends."

"That's not my doing."

Susan scuffed the floor with the toe of her Reeboks. "I don't think you want me to be a real friend to you. I think you just want a little yes-man, a puppet. Someone to keep you company between dates. Someone who'll applaud your little schemes and never question whether the things you do are right. Honestly, I'm ashamed of myself for buying into that for so long."

Daphne drew a ragged breath, but Susan wouldn't let her interrupt.

"It's not friendship when you try to own someone, Daphne. When you have so little faith in them that you view the rest of the world as a threat to your friendship. When you punish them for trying to meet new people. There's nothing wrong with making new friends."

"As long as your 'new friends' aren't creeps." Daphne's eyes were almost pleading. "Susan, Susan. What do you need with those others? Everything used to be so great between us. You, me, buddies forever. That's all I was trying to make you see."

"But I have so much more to give you than just—the way things used to be. If you'd only let me help you . . ."

"I suppose I get the little speech about 'my drinking' now." Daphne tossed her head. "Can you blame me for drinking when my best friend in the world stabs me in the back."

"No way," Susan said, trying to sound more confident than she felt. "No way are you going to lay that on me. You're the one who opens the bottle and pours it, not me."

Daphne glared at her, momentarily speechless. Then she let out a shriek of pure fury. "Ooooh. I just can't believe you're doing this number on me now, Radcliffe. First Scott, then the Gammas, then the Nightingales, and now you. Really, your timing is incredible. Just incredible."

Susan watched in dismay as tears streaked Daphne's face. Still, she held firm.

"I'm afraid you have to take some of the responsibility for those rejections, Daphne."

"Oh, puh-leeze."

"Fine," Susan said. "I can see I'm not accomplishing anything by talking to you now." She started to leave and then turned back. "I just want you to know that I haven't given up on our friendship yet. I'm pretty darn close, but you could still patch things up —if you wanted to. Thing is, you're going to have to ask, and you're going to have to ask nice. I'll stick by you, but I won't trail behind you anymore. And I won't keep my mouth shut if I see you doing something I think is going to hurt someone else—or you."

"So it's your rules or no rules? Is that it?"

"Hey, turn and turn about. We've been playing by your rules up to now and look where it's gotten us."

Susan moved to the door.

"And what if I decide your friendship's not worth it?" Daphne shouted after her, her voice tinged with desperation.

"Then it's not worth it," Susan answered softly, closing the door behind her.

To her surprise, Bruce was standing in the hallway.

"Just couldn't wait to gloat, could you?" she snarled. "I'll bet you think this is a big cause for celebration." Susan tried to shoulder past him, but he had grabbed her arms.

"Susan, I didn't mean to . . . I was just looking for you and I happened to overhear—"

"Let me go," Susan demanded.

"Look at me." Bruce forced her to meet his eyes. "What happened between you and Daphne isn't a good thing. It's a sad thing and I'm sorry. If anything, I really admire you for sticking by Daphne. If I had stuck by *my* friend a little better, maybe he wouldn't have cracked himself up in that car."

"No, don't say that," Susan said, overcome with tenderness. She took Bruce's face between her palms. "I'm sure you were a good friend to him. Hey, you've already been a good friend to me, in spite of all our spats."

Bruce grinned sheepishly.

Susan sighed.

"You want to be alone now?" he asked softly.

"I'm sorry, but I really do."

"I understand," he said, and giving her a quick hug, he let her go.

Susan walked slowly back to her room, relieved to find it empty. She looked at the

ashtray filled with Daphne's menthol cigar-
ettes. Then she threw herself on the bed and
cried.

Chapter 16

"I tell you, I don't know what it means," Susan said as she looked once more at the invitation. "It better be good, though. The boy owes me."

"Don't move your head," Betty cautioned, deftly combing Susan's hair. "French braiding is hard enough without you jiggling around."

Susan was sitting on the floor of her bedroom. Betty leaned over her from the bed, surrounded by clips, rubber bands, hair-setting gel, and fancy combs. As Rachel watched this whole production from her own bed, she shook now and then with amusement.

"Let me see that invitation," Rachel demanded. "Hand it over."

Susan surrendered it reluctantly. "It's so neat, I hate to let it out of my sight."

"You've been looking at it ever since it came this morning," Betty said, beginning her braiding. "You must have it committed to memory by now."

"Oh, I have. *Mr. Bruce Shetland requests the*

honor of your presence at dinner this evening. Eight o'clock. Black tie optional."

Rachel squinted at the card. "And what does this say? The part with the bad handwriting on it?"

Susan laughed. "*At last you will be fed.* Private joke."

"Trust Bruce to go to all the trouble of having an invitation printed up and then writing on it," Rachel said as she handed it back.

"I think it's romantic," Betty sighed as she put the finishing touches on Susan's hair.

"So you wouldn't mind getting something like this from Jorge," Susan teased.

Betty blushed even harder than usual. Susan hoped she hadn't gone too far. And that Betty wasn't taking this Jorge thing too seriously.

Rachel got up and went over to the closet. "Of course, no guy is smart enough to figure a girl needs time to shop for a date like this."

"Actually," Susan said, "I'd hoped I could do my shopping at Pirnie's Resale Shop."

"Nothing's for sale, but we do lend and lease." Rachel pulled a simple white cotton number out of the closet. "What about this?"

Susan looked up intently. "Too sweet, I think."

Rachel nodded. "Gotcha. Don't want to be sweet tonight. What about this?"

Betty and Susan exchanged glances. The gold lamé dress that hung on the hanger was very sexy. What there was of it.

"Too small," Susan said.

"You mean it's the wrong size?"

"Not exactly. What else have you got?"

Rachel pulled out yet another garment. "I don't wear this very often, it's awfully dressy, and it's very delicate."

"Oh, Rachel," Susan gasped. "It's gorgeous."

"I got it at a store that specializes in Art Deco stuff, jewelry and clothes. It's a real Flapper dress. All the beadwork is hand-done, too."

Susan fingered the material. It was just a little slip of a thing. A shimmering, sleeveless black dress with black and white beading. "Can I try it on?"

"Wait a second," Betty said, finishing up the second braid. "There, you're done."

Susan tried on the dress while Rachel and Betty ohhed and ahhed.

"You look like a model," Betty said.

"It's perfect," Rachel agreed, "but if you hurt it, I'll kill you."

"I won't, I promise."

"Then it's yours for tonight."

"Yippee!"

"Let's get it off her, Betty. She's going to ruin it before she gets off the second floor."

Two hours later, as Susan was putting the finishing touches on her makeup, Agatha Mitchell called excitedly down the hall, "There's a stretch limo outside the dorm!"

All down the floor, girls came falling out of their rooms and running to the end of the hall. They huddled around the windows that faced the street. Even Susan put down her mascara brush to come out and look.

"Someone in a tux is coming in here," one of the girls squealed.

Then the buzzer in Susan's room rang.

Betty looked at Susan. "It must be Bruce."

Susan was expecting a nice dinner, but she hardly thought her date was going to start out like this. "I'd better put on my shoes," she said with dignity. Then she ran to grab her silver heels.

Susan was the object of more than one awed stare as she said good-night. There had been plenty of guys coming and going in this dorm all year, but none of them had picked up their dates in a stretch limo.

"Have a good time," Rachel said, along with a chorus of other girls.

Susan had seen Bruce just yesterday, but she was still nervous when she went to greet him in the lounge. First of all, there were as many gaping girls ringing the entryway as there had been upstairs. Then there was Bruce himself. Classy was not a word Susan would normally have associated with Bruce, but standing there, in a black tuxedo, with a white silk scarf draped casually around his neck, he looked like a million bucks. Still, she was relieved to see he had that same silly, crooked grin.

"Susan, you look beautiful," he said, coming over to her.

"You do too," she said.

He held out a red rose. "I hope it won't mess up those braids if you put this in your hair for me."

She smiled up at him. "I'd love to." She went over to the mirror and tucked the rose carefully into the barrette that linked the braids together. "How's that?"

"Perfect."

Suddenly Susan examined Bruce from head to toe. "Wait a minute. You're dressed perfectly."

Bruce preened. "Of course I'm dressed perfectly."

"No, I mean, you don't have one crazy piece of clothing on. It's your trademark."

Without saying a word, Bruce lifted his pants leg. There, peeking over his black formal shoes, were white sweat socks.

"I feel better," Susan said. "We can go now."

As they approached the limo the chauffeur stepped out of the driver's seat and opened the door for Susan and Bruce. Yet another surprise awaited inside. There, on a little shelf next to the open bar was a portable backgammon set. It was all arranged and ready to go.

Susan gave Bruce a dazzling smile. "The car is leased for the whole evening." He shrugged. "I figured we ought to get some use out of it."

As they played a leisurely game of back-gammon, their driver took them on a romantic tour of Boston. They drove along the water and in the harbor area and down some quaint Boston streets.

"I bet I know where we're going for dinner," Susan said.

"I bet you don't. What do you want to bet?"

"Double or nothing on the next game."

"Great," Bruce said, shaking her hand. "Where are we going?"

"Le Bec Fin."

Bruce chortled as he poured each of them some more champagne from the little bar. "I knew you'd say that. I once had a terrible date there. I'm not going back to Le Bec Fin."

Susan experienced a moment's panic. "You didn't get me all dressed up to go to Bruno's, did you?"

"Hardly. This is where we're going."

"There's nothing here," Susan said, looking out the window at a big empty meadow that overlooked the city.

The chauffeur helped them out of the car. "Come with me," Bruce said mysteriously.

Taking his hand, Susan followed Bruce as he walked toward flowering chestnut trees. There she saw a lace-bedecked, beautifully set candlelit table for two.

"I don't believe this," Susan laughed.

"Do you believe this?" A strolling violinist appeared from behind the chestnut trees playing Billy Joel's "I Love You Just the Way You Are."

Bruce swept her in his arms and started dancing.

"You planned all this?" Susan asked, moved almost to tears.

"Of course. You said I never fed you properly, so I said to myself, 'Bruce,' I said, 'why should we go to some crowded noisy restaurant when I can give Susan a night to remember.'"

"You're too much," she said, burying her head in his neck. "How did I ever find you?"

He stroked her hair. "Just lucky, I guess."

Betty Berke sat in the tiny park that butted up against Windsor Hall. Gazing at the stars, she wondered what Susan and Bruce were doing now. Probably dancing, she thought, and Bruce would be holding Susan close. Betty could almost hear the music, but it wasn't Susan and Bruce she was seeing. In her dream she was dancing with Jorge, his strong arms surrounding her as they swayed together.

CRAZY FOR LOVE!

☐ **MIRROR IMAGE by Barbara Bartholomew.** Tired of tagging along after her pretty and popular twin sister, would a summer at her great-aunt's Oklahoma farm bring Brooke a special friend of her own? (139852—$2.50)

☐ **MEET SUPER DUPER RICK MARTIN by Judith Enderle.** Rick's new at Lawrence High and to Annie he's G-O-R-G-E-O-U-S! Only Linda has eyes for him too, and unlike Annie *she* knows how to bat them, *she* knows how to flirt. But Annie's best friend has a plan to get them together that seems foolproof, but is it?   (138686—$2.50)

☐ **JULIE'S MAGIC MOMENT by Barbara Bartholomew.** Julie had never been popular before, but now that she has the lead in the fall play at her new school, everybody wants to know her. As long as she played the roles these new friends expected, Julie would be popular—but what if she stopped pretending?   (126289—$2.25)

☐ **SMART GIRL by Sandy Miller.** Now that she was a senior in high school, Elizabeth Ellen, "E.E.," to her friends, was getting tired of being seen only as the class brain. Then she met handsome Bruce Johnson, and when he asked her out, she realized that though she was bright in school she had a lot to learn about people.   (118871—$2.25)

☐ **FREDDIE THE THIRTEENTH by Sandy Miller.** The dumbest thing pretty Freddie Oliver ever did was tell Bart Cunningham that she had only one sister—when she is really the thirteenth child in a very noisy but loving family of sixteen kids! Will Bart still want to take her out when he discovers the truth?   (134214—$2.25)

Prices slightly higher in Canada
